FRAT BOY
and Toppy

A Theta Alpha Gamma Story

BY ANNE TENINO

D1371961

RIPTIDE
PUBLISHING

Riptide Publishing
PO Box 6652
Hillsborough, NJ 08844
www.riptidepublishing.com

Frat Boy and Toppy

Cover Art and layout by L.C. Chase, http://www.lcchase.com
Editor: Rachel Haimowitz

ISBN: 978-1-937551-30-8

First edition
March, 2012

Also available in ebook
ISBN: 978-1-937551-27-8

FRAT BOY
and Toppy

A THETA ALPHA GAMMA STORY

BY ANNE TENINO

Table of Contents

For Mores.

Chapter 1

One of Brad's frat brothers bent over naked in the locker room showers early one Thursday morning, and he thought, "I'd tap that."

He stood there frozen, skin stinging from the pelletized water, soap suds streaming down his chest while his world made a . . . What did they call that? Paradigm shift.

Dammit, dammit, *dammit*. He'd been trying to avoid this. Admitting it to himself. Consciously. His subconscious had been admitting it for a while in his sleep. *Emitting* it.

Brad flicked another quick look at Collin. Yeah, he still had a delectable ass. *Dammit*.

Brad had spent years trying to avoid the "G" word, but denial was suddenly circling the drain. He stared at the water pouring down at his feet, and thought about hanging on to the security that came with telling himself he wasn't into guys. But it was pointless, right? It wasn't going to go away. Trying not to know it now was like trying to make the soap suds go back in the bar.

He'd tried girls, lots of them, alcohol (even more of that), and running himself ragged. Waited to grow out of it. Looked like maybe he'd grown into it instead. He'd been doing all right his first couple of years at college, but this last year things had gotten difficult.

He'd started having dreams again a few weeks ago, like he'd had when he'd started high school. About naked guys and hard dicks and touching skin. Waking up with sticky sheets. Lately nothing helped with the dreams, not even tequila, but he could sort of ignore them. If he worked at it. Blame it on a fucked-up childhood or something. Pheromone poisoning from spending too much time in the locker room.

Lusting after a guy's wet, hairy, naked ass while awake? Not as easy to avoid noticing.

This isn't the first wet, hairy, naked male ass you've checked out in the shower.

Shit. It wasn't.

Brad heaved a sigh. Water ran from his temples to his chin like a curtain of tears. Except not. He didn't really feel like crying about it. He sort of just felt like . . . dealing with it.

Somehow, a while after Collin and the other guys had finished up and wandered out of the showers and back to their lockers to dress, Brad finally made himself move again. He rinsed off—he wasn't sure what he'd washed and what he hadn't, but who the hell cared? He made it to his locker, but once there, he sort of stalled out, standing there in his boxers and a clean T-shirt, staring blankly at the pair of jeans in his hands.

"Brad, you all right?"

Brad startled when Collin asked that from behind him. "Yeah," he answered automatically. "Fine. Just . . . thinking about a paper."

That was a lame excuse. He never thought about homework unless he had to and everyone knew it. He started pulling on his jeans like everything was normal, and after a few silent seconds, Collin went on his way.

Brad didn't actually know what he'd been thinking about. His brain had mutinied, and he couldn't make sense of all the things swirling around in there. On autopilot, he got dressed and went to his history class.

He hated history. He never would have taken it, but he needed one more humanities class to graduate next year, and his roommate Kyle was taking Classical Greece and had promised to help Brad through it.

In spite of the fact that Professor Whitehall was just as annoying as every other humanities professor out there—fake semi-British accent, amusing little stories about summer trips to Europe, peppering his lectures with foreign phrases—Brad found himself in every class. Even when Kyle didn't go. Wanted to just . . . be there.

It wasn't until Brad was sitting in history that morning, on the south side of the room in the first third of the auditorium just like always, that he even realized he could deny his revelation. Just pretend it had never happened. He wasn't attracted to guys. Couldn't be. He was a jock.

Although there were pro players out there who were gay. They all came out after they retired, but they came out. He was nowhere near pro caliber. No auto-out for him by being a jock.

Maybe he wasn't *completely* gay. Was that possible? Could he be bi?

Brad looked at the table in front of him from between his forearms, tunneling his fingers through his buzz-cut one more time. He rested his forehead on the heels of his hands and closed his eyes.

He needed to think. Just think. Slow down the brain tornado and focus.

He was still trying to get his head to settle down when Ashley Waylon sat down next to him. He could tell it was her even though she didn't say anything. Her perfume, for one thing. It would choke a horse, she laid it on so thick. Brad had dated her for a few boring-as-hell weeks, so he was pretty familiar with it.

I used her for cover. It made his stomach churn. If someone did that to one of his sisters, he'd kick the guy's ass.

I'm scum.

Not that he'd done Ashley—he'd managed not to have sex with any girl in quite a while. He'd been telling himself for years he didn't like girls that were "easy." *Maybe that should have been a clue, numbnuts.* He closed his eyes in disgust, rubbing his head. He'd asked out Ashley when she'd refused to sleep with his frat brother Julian because (according to Julian) she was a "good, Christian girl who was saving herself for marriage."

Virgin girls were rarer than unicorns at Calapooya College and twice as hard to catch. Finding a girl who didn't expect him to try to sleep with her was gold. Brad had heard Julian bitching about Ashley and known she was the girl for him. At least, she would be until she got sick of his unenthusiastic attitude toward her and dumped him. Which was what usually happened.

That hadn't worked as planned with Ashley, though. When Brad had discovered she indeed did want to have sex, very much so, he was forced to do the dumping.

Brad stilled when it hit him. *That's when this all started up again.* Right after the beginning of winter term, when he'd broken up with Ashley. He'd felt restless and trapped and bored and he wanted out of what could barely be called a relationship because, whenever he saw Ashley, he felt like he was wearing wool long-johns: itchy all over.

After they'd broken up, he'd started having the dreams again.

Brad remembered Ashley's actual presence when her pink-lacquered nails wrapped around his forearm. "Brad?" Her voice was the practiced honey of a boyfriend-hunter. "Sweetie? Are you all right?"

"No. I'm gay." There, he'd said it. His heart tried to gallop right out of his chest. He heard sudden rustling in front of him. Like someone was turning around to stare. Brad's stomach swooped down low and balled itself up tight. Whoops, guess that guy knew now, too.

Ashley laughed. "Oh, Brad!" She hit him softly in the shoulder. "You're so funny! I swear; always kidding."

No. Not really, actually. He wasn't known for his sense of humor. He dropped one arm and turned to look at her, temple on his palm now. "You think I'm kidding?" He could hear the slight snarl in his voice.

Ashley began to look unsure, losing her smile and sucking her lower lip into her mouth. "Of course," she answered. She nodded for emphasis.

Brad opened his mouth, but came to his senses just in time. "Well, yeah, course I am." He rustled up a fake smile for her. Then he straightened up and eyed the guy in front of him, who was eyeing him right back. Brad stared. The guy turned around.

Being a big, imposing football player had its uses.

"Brad, I was thinking maybe we could get together for coffee sometime." Ashley was twirling her finger in her hair. Didn't girls know that was a dead giveaway? "Hang out, you know. Just friends." She was leaning toward him, keeping her voice down. Brad glanced at the guy in front of him again. He was leaning as far back in his chair as possible. If his ears were on stalks they'd be waving in Brad's face.

"I'm not sure I'm ready for that yet." He kept his voice gentle. "It's only been a couple of weeks since, you know, I told you I needed some alone time." Brad looked away, overcome by being a lying sack of shit. He turned back, putting on his "brave" face, and shrugged.

"You're a great girl. If I were ready for a real relationship . . . but I'm not." He gave her his broken-hearted smile.

That "real relationship" line was so useful. He didn't know what the fuck it meant, but his older sister Ellie told him to use it, and it worked. She'd said if he was going to go through girls like toilet paper, he should at least try and mitigate the damage. "You bastard," she'd added.

Ashley was all overdone sympathy. She shook her head sadly, looking soulfully into Brad's eyes. "Oh, Brad," she said in that sugary way. "I understand. You just let me know when you're ready for the next step."

Brad groaned internally. He was in a fucking soap opera. "I can't even think about it. I'm not ready. Gives me anxiety attacks." He rubbed his chest, as if he had a tightness there and could massage it away.

She finally subsided. Looking troubled and a little bit pouty, but trying to hide it. "Well, you know if you ever want to try it again. Or, you know, if I can do anything for you . . ."

"Man, Ashley, thanks. I really need someone to take notes today. I kind of have a headache. That's what I was doing when you sat down."

If there was a hell, he was headed there.

"Sure!" She was like an annoying little bird. Feed the damn things once and they just keep coming back.

If someone thought that about one of my sisters, I'd kick his ass.

Chapter 2

Brad was in a daze. He didn't know what was going on but he could hear Whitehall droning on, and pens scratching on paper. Someone typing on a keyboard behind him. He let it all wash over him. White noise. Eventually he managed some kind of zoned-out calm. More forgetfulness than Zen. His head on the desk, chin resting on his fists.

An hour into Professor Whitehall's lecture on Pallas Athena (whoever the fuck that was), Professor Whitehall's aide, Sebastian, walked in with a stack of papers—their last batch of essays, maybe—and set them down on the desk at the side of the room. Brad's brain woke up a little to watch; he always had a good view of Sebastian from this seat. Whitehall lectured from the podium on the stage, and Sebastian's desk was down low and off to the side. People probably didn't even notice Sebastian.

He noticed Sebastian. There was something about him Brad couldn't seem to *stop* noticing. Maybe it was the way he was always so perfect-looking. Not in a stuffy way. Just . . . put together. His T-shirts never had stains, and they always fit him, and if he had holes in his jeans you knew they were there on purpose. His hair was always perfect. Not like he put a bunch of crap in it, but just there, and dark and kinda short, choppy, freshly brushed. It never stuck up in the back like he'd been drinking 'til all hours with the guys and rolled out of bed thirty seconds before he had to leave for class.

Sebastian had cool shoes, too. Like Vans or Chuck Taylor's or other sorta retro stuff. Today he was wearing his pink high-tops. His jeans were classic, almost too baggy, but his really tight T-shirt made up for it. Jesus, he had to work for abs like that, didn't he? That couldn't be natural.

Brad shrugged to himself, almost dislodging his chin from his fist. Maybe Sebastian's abs were natural. Brad was used to guys who went to fat if they didn't work out—that's how most of his frat buddies were—but Sebastian probably wasn't that kind of guy. He wasn't slim exactly, just not bulky. He was trim. Lame word, but whatever. Fit. Tight. Well made.

That's how come Sebastian had abs like that. Damn, they just looked so solid under that shirt. Maybe sometime Brad could get a better look at them. He let his eyes drift closed, falling into some kind of vision where Sebastian's naked torso was under his hands. He could trace those muscles, see just how cut the guy was. Did he have chest hair? In Brad's head, he did. Lots of it, all black and swirling in toward his sternum. Brad pushed his fingers through the hair, tracing the lower edge of a pec. A pinkish brown nipple peeked out at him. He let his hand fall slowly to Sebastian's abdominal muscles. Six-pack. Oh, eight-pack. And those muscles that cut in right over his hips that gave guys that beautiful V shape. He ran a hand down one of those, and whoa. Sebastian was naked.

Brad's eyes popped open.

Holy.

Fucking.

Shit.

He *was* gay. And hard as a railroad spike.

He'd kind of thought that might be the case.

It settled into him, coating him and soaking into his skin. Like metal filings on a magnet. Oil on plastic. Marinara on a white T-shirt. Homosexuality seemed to have taken a liking to him, and it wasn't likely to wash out.

ΘΑΓ

Sebastian made no effort to learn the names and faces of the students in the lower-level history class he was the TA for. He knew the history majors from repeated contact, but the other people weren't going to feature in his life past these three months, so he didn't bother.

Which was why it surprised him when his brain automatically supplied the name of the hot jock who always sat next to Kyle (Medieval History, class of 2013). When Kyle bothered to show up.

Fucking undergrad history majors.

Sebastian's brain was kind of insistent on returning to Hot Guy, so he put Kyle out of his mind. Brad (a.k.a. Hot Guy) had turned in a paper this week. Smart. He'd be one of the people who wasn't scrambling at the end of term to write and hand in all the required papers during finals week. Probably Kyle's influence. In Sebastian's experience, frat boys and jocks weren't generally the kind to do the homework today that they could put off for nine weeks.

He watched Brad walk up to the desk and turn in this week's essay, shuffling along in the line of other students. Watched Brad fairly openly, but Brad never looked at him. As if he was trying really hard not to.

Whatever, it was fine. Because Brad was nice to look at, and Sebastian didn't need to deal with some pissed-off frat boy jock feeling like he'd been violated because the gay guy appreciated his muscles. And his cheekbones. Brad had high, prominent ones.

That was the nice thing about man-watching. Each one had something unique Sebastian could appreciate. Sometimes he had to look a little harder than other times, but . . . yeah. Brad had unique cheekbones.

And beautiful musculature, coming or going, he thought as Brad walked away.

On his way back to his office, Sebastian dug out Brad's essay. *Brad Feller.* Just Brad? Not Bradley? Sebastian might have to look on the class attendance roster. Somehow, Hot Guy looked like a Bradley to him.

Chapter 3

The next Tuesday, Brad dragged Kyle's ass to class. If Brad had to take notes, he couldn't imagine what would happen. There'd be no fucking notes was what would happen. Figuring out you were gay made it difficult to concentrate on Classical Greece. In spite of all the queers floating around back then.

Figuring out you were gay made it difficult to concentrate on much of anything. Although he'd sort of managed a decent attitude about it the last couple days. Achieved some equilibrium.

Kind of.

Dragging Kyle to class was easy, actually. Kyle was worried about him. The whole fucking frat was worried about him. Everyone was worried because Brad hadn't hooked up in over a month. Hadn't even tried to fake it. Even El Presidente Eduardo, who saw Brad as his main competition when it came to "the ladies," was worried. In his own special way.

Ashley didn't seem worried about him, though. She was sitting totally on the other side of the auditorium. Thank God. Brad shook his head at himself for the hundredth time since last week. He still didn't understand what he'd been thinking when he went out with her. Or all the girls before her.

For some stupid reason, he'd thought he needed an image as a player when he started college, and he'd begun cultivating it as soon as he'd arrived by hooking up with lots of girls. Or at least seeming to. Most of the time he was fronting for his image, but he'd had years to perfect his act. No one ever seemed to suspect anything.

Brad was no competition for ol' Eddie, that was for sure. Unless Eduardo was chasing the same brand of tail, and Brad was pretty damn sure he wasn't. 'Course, most guys would say the same about him, he figured.

He snorted softly to himself and caught Kyle's swift look out of the corner of his eye. Brad's whole image was lame. He had to be nearly falling-down drunk to touch a girl now. Why women chased him was a mystery. He was a complete asshole to them. Shit, he wasn't even that good-looking. He had a mirror; he could see it was true.

He was suddenly seeing a lot of things that were true about himself.

Among all the other revelations last week, Brad figured out he was attracted to dark-haired guys with tight, compact bodies. Like Sebastian's. He wanted guys on the short side, with hairy chests and thighs and even hair on their ass. Maybe because he had so little body hair.

His palms tingled just thinking about body hair.

He needed some shoulder, a nice meaty ass, but yeah, compact. It got his motor running. He'd faked being sick all weekend so he could skip the frat's morning workouts and do some internet "research" on the subject. He'd spent a lot of time looking at clips of guys who looked kind of like Sebastian. The best ones were when the guys who looked like Sebastian paired up with guys who looked kind of like himself. Most of the dreams he'd been having since he broke up with Ashley had featured a guy who looked a lot like Sebastian.

That was when he first started thinking maybe being gay wouldn't be so bad. His reaction to straight porn was pretty much a yawn, but show him two (or more) guys getting it on? He'd never jerked off so many times in a row in his life. Not even when he was fifteen.

He'd been kind of surprised to find out he wanted a guy who wore glasses.

Sebastian had glasses, but he only wore them when he was reading something.

Sebastian looked really smart in those glasses.

Brad wanted to see Sebastian wearing those glasses and looking down on him. Unzipping his jeans and reaching in, letting him—

Kyle jostled Brad's arm. Brad looked at him. Kyle was looking back with concern. "Wha'?"

"You all right, dude?" Kyle whispered. "You made a weird noise."

"What kinda noise?" Brad whispered back.

"You sounded kinda sick. I dunno. Like a dying mouse."

Brad narrowed his eyes and stared until Kyle sighed and went back to his note-taking. Prof Whitehall was still yammering away up there.

Right on time, Sebastian walked in to pick up the weekly essays. Brad's whole body tightened up, but he fought to hold his nonchalant, head-on-desk pose. He tracked Sebastian with his eyes, though. Like a bird dog or something.

Fuck. Okay, he needed to take some action here. Needed to get Sebastian's attention. He had plenty of experience with girls; how different could it be? He knew Sebastian was gay, everyone did. The thought of being with Sebastian . . .

Shit. He'd made that noise again.

Chapter 4

Brad was such a dumbass sometimes. He almost hit himself in the forehead. But if he'd done that, he would've missed what Ty and Sloan were saying. He forced away the "gay jocks!" moment and concentrated.

"What, that little Sebastian dude?" Sloan was asking.

"Ain't nothing little about him," Ty said in a smug voice. Brad scowled into his locker, where he was pretending to look for something.

"That boy gets around. You're like the fourth guy this month who told me they got with him."

Brad stilled. Four guys? In a *month*? That was like . . . like him with girls. At least according to the carefully nurtured rumors.

Okay, so the good news was that Sebastian was easy. Well fuck, he was a guy. Wasn't "easy" in the definition?

Brad missed the next couple of things Ty and Sloan said as they slammed their lockers shut and moved toward the showers. Then he heard Sloan's voice again, drifting away. "I can't believe you bottomed for that little dude."

"Telling you, ain't nothing little."

Brad's gut tightened so suddenly he lost his breath. He flushed hot and cold and broke into a sweat. Sebastian was a top? Brad's ass clenched up tight. Not in a this-is-the-US-Mint-and-you-aren't-getting-in kinda way, either. His blood started pounding in various extremities, and he had to lean his forehead against the cool metal inside his locker door.

"Hey," Kyle said, coming up behind him. Brad jumped, just a little. Hopefully Kyle didn't notice. "What the hell's taking you so long, man? We're all in the weight room but you."

Brad turned to look at Kyle, and the compulsion to tell him just *exactly* what was taking him so long was so overwhelming he opened his mouth. But even though he was pretty sure Kyle wouldn't freak out (much), and Brad knew he'd have to tell him—*knew* he was going to tell the whole frat eventually—what came out was, "Do you know Ty Broca and Sloan Tines?"

Kyle looked at him weird for a second, trying to judge what was up. He'd been looking at Brad that way a lot since that Thursday afternoon a couple weeks ago. "No." He shrugged. When Brad just looked at him, he went on. "They're in track." He leaned forward and added in a whisper, "And they're fags." Because Ty and Sloan might be fags, but they were tall, built fags with big muscles and a supportive frat behind them.

Would Brad's frat be supportive? Could he join Ty and Sloan's as a senior? Did he fucking care? "I think you're supposed to say 'gay,' dude." Brad slammed his locker shut. He needed to get some exercise and stop thinking so Goddamned much. "C'mon, stop talking and let's go."

Kyle made a face at him and followed Brad out of the locker room.

ΘΔΓ

Sebastian was a top. He stuck his dick up other guys' stretched, lubed asses and . . . *oh God*.

When Brad had started checking out gay porn, he was a little surprised to always find himself identifying with the guy getting fucked. It made his asshole twitch and the muscles in his butt contract the first time he watched some guy push his dick into another guy's tiny little hole, stretching him wide and smoothing out all those little puckers.

Brad wanted to know what it felt like, so he'd done a little experimenting after he'd started the gay porn fest. He wasn't about to go buy a dildo, but finding a penis-shaped object lying around was, like, no work at all. He got off, of course, thanks to ol' Lefty (or was it Hairy?) but it was uncomfortable having something inside him. It made all his hairs stand up, all over his body. Made him feel like he had to take a dump.

He wasn't so into it. Except doing it once had created this kind of *itch* inside of him. And even though he knew it wasn't that great, he'd been sorta obsessed with it. Like, to the point where he was lying awake at 2 a.m. almost squirming after having heard Ty and Sloan in the locker room. The muscles in his ass were throbbing at him. From his sphincter to somewhere just south of his belly button, they *wanted*. It nearly drove him nuts.

Brad got up and locked himself in the bathroom, surreptitiously carrying the hairbrush with the perfect handle. How was he going to explain the need to brush his hair at 2:38? It was less than an inch long; he could barely explain the need to brush it at all. He didn't even own a hairbrush.

Hopefully, Kyle would never notice it missing.

It had ridges ringing the handle. This time, Brad took more time working it into himself. His brain must have had some idea he was going to try this again, because he'd picked up KY. It seemed to work better than the lotion he'd stolen from Kyle last time.

And fuck, even though he knew it was going to be uncomfortable, that first touch of his lube-smeared finger sliding across his hole, feeling the little puckers . . . Brad shuddered and shivered and nearly moaned with it.

No moaning. He bit his lip, hard.

The tapered end of the brush slid in, stretching him—okay, that felt fucking good. He'd had no idea he was so sensitive there. He took his time, pushing in, pulling out in tiny increments. He felt each one of those rings slip past his sphincter, and every time one stretched him wider and then slipped in, releasing some of that pressure but still *there*, he felt it zing up his spine.

When it was in up to the bristles, he lay there panting and feeling shaky, skin prickling with the feel of something foreign in there, breaking out in a sweat. He still just didn't know if he *liked* it. Somehow, though, it lit him up inside. Especially when he closed his eyes and pictured Sebastian's face hanging over his.

Tentatively, he touched the hairbrush, moving it slightly. *Oh fuck.*

He was starting to see how this could feel good.

His skin still crawled a little, and he still felt like he was being sort of invaded, but he wanted it. Craved it. In a very physical way— needing more of that feeling of being filled and the sliding touch into his asshole and against the muscle inside. *Smooth muscle*, his brain told him. Like he fucking cared. Oh, God, and that was his prostate one of those ridges had just slid slowly across.

A small noise escaped him, and the last of the uncertainty about how much he wanted this dissolved into sensation. Brad felt like something was blooming inside him. It felt so good he didn't even make fun of himself when he was hit with the image of his ass opening up like a flower.

So he fucked himself with the handle of a hair brush while he jerked off, lying on the bathroom floor. He bit his lip so hard trying to be quiet that he could taste blood on his tongue as he arched into his hands and shuddered out one of the best orgasms of his life. The muscles in his asshole clamped down on the thing inside of him, and he bit down harder to keep from crying out.

He sprawled out spread-eagled on the bathroom floor, panting, spooge all over his belly, hairbrush up his ass. Little shocks pinging around every few seconds, then tapering off. He opened his eyes and looked at the light above him. A wave of affection for the little bathroom with the stupid goldenrod wallpaper and the too-bright fluorescent light almost brought tears to his eyes. He lifted a shaky hand and swiped his mouth with his forearm. It came away with a streak of blood, and even that was enough to cause a little shudder.

Brad sighed and closed his eyes again. *I'm so gay.*

Chapter 5

"**C**'mon, dude. Just tell me. Is it an STD?"

That got Brad's attention. "What?" Kyle had been yammering at him for a few minutes, but Brad was working on his history essay. It had to be really good. He was positive the person who actually read these was Sebastian, and if he wanted Sebastian's attention, one way to get it was to write a memorable essay. One that was memorable because it was so good.

Kyle was fucking with his concentration. The history of Sparta took some effort to write about. It was boring as hell. Nothing about guys-on-guys in the books he was looking in.

"Do you have some kinda STD? Is that why you aren't the Alpha Dawg anymore?"

God, were these guys ever gonna get past this? "No. And I fucking hate that nickname. Go away, I'm trying to write."

"And what's with that, dude? You hate history."

"I still gotta pass it, Kyle. If I don't keep up the GPA, I lose the scholarship."

"Yeah, but you usually write some lame-ass paper on Monday night. You've been working on that one for, like, five hours and it's freaking Saturday. You get high enough grades in your other classes to even it all out." Kyle refrained from mentioning most of those classes were health, PE, and "family and consumer sciences." Home ec, in other words.

Brad shrugged. *Whatever.* "I want it to be good." The fuck was a *stoa* again? Kyle stood silently next to him for so long Brad had to look up again. "What?"

"All you need's a C. Why do you care if it's good?"

Dammit. Brad looked back down at his paper again, quickly. "Just do," he muttered, flipping through his book like he was looking up something very important.

Kyle sighed and walked a couple steps away to flop down on his bed. "The guys are starting a betting pool, Brad."

"Why do I care?"

"It's about you. They're taking bets on how long you can go without getting laid, and why you stopped chasing tail."

"Huh."

"Tank bet you're secretly engaged."

Brad laughed. "Yeah? He's gonna lose."

"Ricky bet two hundred bucks that you're secretly engaged with a baby on the way." Brad could tell by the sound of Kyle's voice he was smiling over that one.

Brad sighed. "No one ever claimed Ricky was smart. What are the odds?"

"Shit, I don't know. I never understood how that worked."

"So who bet I have an STD?"

Kyle didn't answer. Which was sort of an answer in itself. "Hope you didn't put a lot of money on that, bro," Brad murmured without looking around.

Kyle huffed a breath out. "Collin laid twenty on you being gay." He started laughing.

Brad froze up for just a second. Kyle's laughter didn't change, so he must not have noticed. Brad forced a big grin and turned around. He even managed a chuckle or two. "Hope he didn't need that twenty."

He was going to have to keep an eye on Collin.

ΘΑΓ

Brad got a C+ on his paper about Sparta. Sebastian didn't even look at him when he handed it back.

The next week, Brad bought a paper online.

The following Tuesday, two days early, Sebastian walked in and straight up to Brad, handing his paper back while Prof Whitehall was yakking away. Sebastian barely looked at him when he dropped it in front of Brad. It had a sticky note on it. Once Brad got over seeing Sebastian walk straight toward him, and then checking out his ass as Sebastian walked away, he read the note.

2:30 p.m., my office, rm 232a Allen

Whose office? Prof Whitehall's? Brad broke out in a cold sweat and leaned over to hiss into Kyle's ear, "Where's Whitehall's office?"

Kyle was starting to get used to Brad's weird new quirks. He barely glanced at Brad before writing "History Dept." on the margin of his notepaper. Brad nudged him and raised his eyebrows. Kyle rolled his eyes and wrote "236 Allen Hall."

So, not Professor Whitehall's office, then. That must mean . . . Sebastian's office? Brad took a deep breath. This time the sweat broke out on his hands. That "Hot for Teacher" song started playing in his head. About a million images flashed through his mind, a lot of them involving him on his knees. His stomach balled up in a knot and all his blood rushed south.

Fuck, fuck, fuck. *Please.*

Class got out at 11:00. He wasn't able to eat lunch, didn't even try. Instead, he went back to the frat and fretted. He didn't have a lot of prior experience with fretting. What did Sebastian want? Could it be the same thing Brad wanted? He finally left his room in a haze and his baggiest pair of jeans at two o'clock.

This must be what it felt like when you were fourteen and had your first crush. Except he was twenty-one, and he'd never felt this way at fourteen. Even then he'd seen girls as mostly status symbols. A necessary evil. He'd been the star running back in a small-town high school. He'd had an image to maintain. His coach had made it very clear he expected that from him.

Brad stood in front of the short hallway to the #232 offices. "A" was the first one on his right. There were four more doors: one more on the right side, two on the left and one at the end. The hallway wasn't well-lit, but he could pretty clearly see the door to 232A was propped open.

Voices drifted out of the open doorway. For just a second, his mind went to that porn video he'd seen over the weekend, where the teachers "punished" that student by tying him down and fucking him over a desk. All of them. An academic gangbang.

Brad swallowed. This wouldn't be like that. Maybe Sebastian had noticed Brad watching him (how could he not?). Maybe he was crazy attracted to Brad, and he was fishing to see if Brad could maybe swing that way.

Oh, he could so fucking swing that way. He'd bend over the desk right now if Sebastian asked him to.

"I have a kind of important meeting." Sebastian's voice, drifting down the hall.

Brad's heart thumped a couple of times, reminding him it needed some oxygen. *That's me.* He started walking toward the door, listening for more. He didn't hear anything else but Sebastian's voice, murmuring. What did he have to say to his officemate in such a quiet voice?

Then Brad was standing in the doorway, clearing his throat. He wasn't doing it to attract Sebastian's attention. He needed to clear it. It was dry as a desert. Sebastian turned toward him at the sound and smiled.

Brad thought he might faint. *Man up, dude.*

"Hey, Brad," Sebastian said, walking his way and smiling that smile.

Brad swallowed. "Hey," he croaked. Sebastian cocked his head a second, studying him. He stopped a couple feet in front of Brad, still looking at him like he was trying to figure something out. "Um, hey, I thought the office was going to be free, but it looks like it's not. I'd kinda like to talk to you in private, so . . ." Sebastian raised an eyebrow at him.

Could this actually be about what Brad wanted it to be about? Like, a hook-up? "Private's good," Brad blurted. Then felt himself go red.

"Yeah," Sebastian agreed immediately. He looked like he was trying not to smile. "Yeah, so I think we can probably find a semi-deserted coffee shop on Sixth Avenue, and probably get a table with enough privacy to talk there."

The *bow-chicka-bow-bow* soundtrack in Brad's head stopped playing. Either the dude was way kinkier than Brad was ready for, or this wasn't going to be about sex.

That's when it hit Brad's testosterone-addled brain what else this meeting might be about.

Chapter 6

"**S**o. Brad. You probably have an idea what I wanted to talk to you about."

"No," he said, unthinkingly. He was watching Sebastian's hands stir and stir and stir and stir his cappuccino. He didn't drink those kinds of drinks, so he wasn't sure if this was normal. Did fancy coffee need more stirring?

The stirring stopped. "No?" Sebastian's voice sounded kinda hard.

Brad looked up from his hands into Sebastian's eyes. They were so brown. Kind of soft, deep brown. Except at the moment they looked a little bit pissed. He dumbly shook his head. Even though, yeah, he was pretty sure he *did* know what this was about. He'd fucked up good.

Sebastian took a deep breath, held it, and let it out slowly. "Okay, let's start here. You're on an athletic scholarship, yeah? And another one from your frat?"

Oh, had Sebastian been checking him out? His heart did some sort of fluttery thing. "Yeah. Not that big a deal. I mean, we're only a smaller Division II school, so it's not like I'm some great player or anything . . ." His voice sort of gave up under Sebastian's intense look.

"And you need those scholarships, right?"

"Well, uh . . ." He ran a hand through his hair and looked out the window. *Shit.* "Yeah. I mean, my parents never could have sent me to a private school otherwise. Not without a lot of debt, you know. I'm the second of five and . . ." He gave up again. He'd made the mistake of looking back at Sebastian and the guy so totally was just waiting for him to shut up. He looked down, not wanting to see that in Sebastian's eyes. But Sebastian's next words snapped Brad's head back up.

"Okay, so bottom line is, if you want to keep your scholarships, you have to rewrite this paper by 8 a.m. Thursday. Otherwise I have to show the one you bought online to Ari."

Brad's mind seized on the one unimportant detail. "Ari?" he croaked.

"Professor Whitehall," Sebastian snapped. Then he leaned forward, even more intense. "Frankly, I shouldn't even be giving you this chance. Athletes are always skating by and it makes me sick. But I've given other students one chance, so you get one, too. You've never done it before, and I'm told it's the end of the football season and that's a high-pressure time for you. You're Goddamned lucky I'm feeling generous."

Brad knew he was bright red. He hung his head. "I know," he whispered. "Sorry." He debated telling Sebastian football season had ended two months ago, but he wasn't sure he'd get it out. *Way to impress him.*

"That wasn't exactly the reaction I expected."

Lost in his own crawling ball of shame, Brad was so startled he almost flinched when Sebastian spoke. He glanced up, not raising his head.

Sebastian had his chin in his hand, looking at him. "You aren't really the stereotypical jock frat boy you look like, are you?"

Brad cleared his throat and thought about his generally uncaring attitude toward people's feelings and his beer-swilling, womanizing, asshole friends. "Uh, yeah. Actually I kinda am." Maybe Sebastian expected him to get mad. He dug way down deep for some mad but came up empty.

He had plenty of "loser" on tap, though.

Sebastian seemed to be smothering a smile behind his hand. Like maybe he was laughing at Brad, but didn't want him to know. Well, at least he'd made an effort. Brad shrugged, feeling his ears go hot again. He looked back down at his hands.

"What do you want to do once you graduate?"

He shrugged again. Mostly he just wanted the fuck out of this coffee shop. About thirty seconds ago. Sebastian waited him out. Brad sighed and glanced up from under his brow at Sebastian. He looked like he was thinking. He always looked like he was thinking. "Something with sports, I guess." Brad shifted. He really, really needed out of this chair.

Sebastian picked up his drink. Somehow, while they'd been sitting there, it had deflated. It just looked like coffee with milk in it now. Some foam clinging to the sides of the cup. Sebastian swirled his coffee while Brad watched his hand. Seemed like maybe he had a thing for hands. He watched Sebastian throw back his head and chug the coffee. The whole thing, like it was a shot or something. Baring his neck. Fuck, he even had a sexy neck.

Who knew? He was a neck-man, too.

Hell, he was just a Sebastian-man.

Sebastian set the empty mug down and looked at Brad. "Just have it to my office by 8 a.m. Thursday, okay? Get Kyle to help you if you need it, he's pretty good at history. *Help* you, not write it for you."

Brad cleared his throat. "'Kay."

Sebastian gave him a tight smile and stood up, walking out of the cafe without looking back. Which might have been good, since even now Brad found Sebastian's ass mesmerizing.

Brad blew out a breath and slumped back once Sebastian was out the door. The chair that he'd been dying to get out of two minutes ago wouldn't let him go now.

It was after he'd knocked his skull into the back of the chair a couple of times that it occurred to Brad to wonder how Sebastian knew he was friends with Kyle. He sat up in surprise. Suddenly the chair was willing to release him.

Ashley, however, was not. He hadn't noticed her there. Had he really been that focused on Sebastian? Probably. Didn't matter, because she was marching toward him like one of those mythical bird-women. What were they called? Harpies.

"Brad," she said, nodding curtly, her hands planted on her hips. She looked pretty . . . militant. "I'd like to talk to you, if you have a minute."

"Ashley, I kinda have t—"

"Buy me a coffee. I'll be sitting over there, waiting for you. Light cream." She tossed her hair and marched off.

He considered his options for all of two seconds.

She knew where to find him.

He bought the coffee. Then he put a splash of cream in it. It looked almost white. He stuck the lid back on, in case that wasn't the right amount of cream.

He approached the table cautiously, holding the coffee in front of him. She looked like some offended Greek goddess. He hoped his offering would please her. Or at least not piss her off further. God knew why he was trying to placate her in the first place.

To make the whole thing end faster. Duh.

She eyed him, snatched the coffee from his hand, peeled off the lid, and inspected the contents. It seemed to be good enough for her to sip, but she gave him a disgruntled look as she did so. Like she'd *wanted* it to be wrong.

She took another sip and stared at the table, lips nearly frozen on the rim of the cup. Brad was starting to wonder if she was having some kind of seizure when she gave a short nasty laugh and muttered, "Who the fuck cares?"

That's what it sounded like to him, at least. If she was going to talk to herself, he was outta here. He cleared his throat at her. Startled, she looked up at him, huffed, and waved at the chair across from her.

After he sat down, he realized he probably should have walked out instead. Whatever. Let her do her thing and then he'd go start on that paper. He was so lucky Sebastian was letting him have a do-over. Now he just had to explain it to Kyle and then—

"How long have you been seeing him?"

"What?" He jerked to look at Ashley again.

"How long have you and Sebastian been together?" She had a nasty smile on her face.

Oh fuck.

"Or maybe you aren't together? Oh, that'd be classic. The guy who has girls falling all over themselves to get his attention can't get the guy he *yearns* for. Poor wittle Bwad. Not good enough for the boy he wuvs."

He'd felt this lightheaded before. In the middle of a football game, right before he'd passed out. He meant to say something, but Ashley went on. "What, you think I can't see you're hot for Sebastian? What was that all about? Did he turn you down? Did you offer him anything he wanted if only he'd just go out with you and he said he wasn't interested?"

That hit a little too close to home. "Ashley, don't fuck with me."

Instead of backing down, like people usually did when he got pissed, she laughed at him, slightly hysterical. "Fuck you, Brad." Ashley smirked at him over the edge of her cup, then took another drink. "I think I just caught your attention more effectively than I did the entire time we went out, didn't I?"

Brad gritted his teeth and stared her down.

She won.

"So, what's everyone going to say when they find out the Calapooya College football star is gay?"

Everything froze inside him as the real danger of Ashley knowing dawned on him.

Was it a danger, really? Was he ready to face everyone knowing? "So. You going to tell everyone?"

Ashley took an aggressive sip of her coffee that somehow reminded him of how angry women in old movies smoked when confronting the man who'd spurned them. Puffing smoke in his face, alternating with hollowing her cheeks, making the cherry glow.

Damn indoor smoking ban, anyway.

Ashley slammed the cup down, sloshing coffee over the edge. She looked out the window. "You're really gay?"

What was his line again? "Uhhhhh . . ."

She stared at him a long time. "I was just pissed. I guess that's what I thought, but I expected you to deny it."

Brad swallowed a couple times.

"Aren't you going to deny it?"

"Well, um . . ."

"So you *are* gay."

"I don't . . . know."

"Are you seeing Sebastian?"

He stared at the table and shook his head.

"But you want to see him? You're attracted to him."

"Yeah," he whispered.

"Are you maybe bi, though?"

"I don't know." *Liar.*

"So, you're attracted to Sebastian. Are you attracted to me?"

"Not, um, not really."

"Sounds gay to me, Brad."

"Kinda does," he managed.

"But you can't say it."

"Not really." He shook his head at the table.

"Shit," Ashley muttered. "I guess if you can't even say it, you aren't really ready to come out. I'm not that big a bitch. Not that . . . mad. I'll keep it to myself."

In a moment of stunning insight—especially for him, considering he was so wrapped up in his own head that his vision was graying—Brad realized maybe Ashley wasn't just angry. She was humiliated. Which reminded him what she had to be humiliated about. He finally looked up at her. She was looking out the window, arms folded across her chest. He cleared his throat and scratched his ear. "I'm sorry."

Ashley looked back at him. "What?"

"I used you. I didn't know it, not at the time. Not exactly. I mean, I knew I wasn't exactly . . . interested, but I didn't realize it was because. Um."

"You're gay?"

Brad closed his eyes but managed a nod.

"So you sort of knew you were using me, but you did it anyway."

He opened one eye and peeked at her. Then he nodded again.

"You're an asshole." She said it without any real anger in her voice. For some reason, his shoulders relaxed. "A confused asshole, but an asshole."

"I am."

"I saw you staring at Sebastian. In class, but also today in here. I was walking by and saw you talking to him and the look on your face. You looked nervous." Ashley curled her lip, sneering out the window. "You're hypnotized by Sebastian's rear whenever he walks away from you. I was pissed off all over again. I'm not stupid." Her voice actually softened some. "But I think you kind of are."

He stared at her. *Huh*?

"I'm mad, and I wish you'd told me when you figured it out. I wish you'd never asked me out. But I guess I kinda believe that you didn't know about being gay. We didn't sleep together, so . . . Just . . .

Brad, you know when I asked you if we could still be friends?" She looked at him.

"Yeah . . ."

"I don't want to be your friend anymore. Right now? I'm so done with you."

"Oh. Okay."

She stood up, nodding sharply at him.

"Ashley," he said as she walked away. She stopped and looked down her nose at him. "I really am sorry." She looked at him a second longer, but didn't say anything when she started walking again.

Chapter 7

"**S**o what, you just let him off?" Paul asked. He was across the office they shared, sitting at his desk, staring over at Sebastian. Backlit by the windows, weak winter sunlight washing in.

Sebastian shrugged. "Yeah." He started pulling the massive stack of student essays out of his locked bottom drawer and let them fall onto his desk. It was a pretty satisfying *slam*. He had them about half done. Truth was, he kind of liked grading the essays. They got pretty amusing.

Paul scowled at him. "Jocks are always getting away with murder, and you just gave away that much power over one?" He had a real aversion to jocks, frat boys, and their ilk.

Sebastian shrugged. He'd have done it for anyone in that class, pretty much. Once. Unless they gave him a lot of shit. Which, if he was honest, he'd expected from Brad. "He didn't react the way I thought he would." Sebastian leaned back in his desk chair and looked out the window, thinking about the look on Brad's face when he'd said *Sorry*. Just how wrong was it that that look had excited him a little bit?

Paul was silent a minute, thinking, so Sebastian let himself have a micro-fantasy. About Brad's naked ass being introduced to his dick.

"What do you mean?" Paul finally asked, a touch annoyed.

Sebastian smiled but hid it by rubbing his chin. "He always comes across as really cocky, you know? Tries to be imposing, never smiles. He was nervous when he showed up, you saw that, yeah? It was completely unlike him."

Paul nodded and waved him on, looking at Sebastian suspiciously.

"I thought he'd get intimidating and confrontational when I told him I knew he hadn't written that paper, but he just, I don't know, folded. I was almost afraid he was going to cry for a couple seconds."

Paul was silent a minute longer, so Sebastian threw his feet up on his desk to wait him out. Paul narrowed his eyes. "How many students are in that class?"

Sebastian grinned, not trying to hide it this time. He'd wondered when this would occur to Paul. "About a hundred."

"And you're there, what, a half-hour a week? You don't even take attendance for Ari, man. You just read all those essays those kids generate."

"Some of those kids are older than me."

"Don't change the subject," Paul snapped.

Sebastian linked his arms across his chest and grinned at the ceiling now. "Yeah, a half-hour a week. I noticed this guy. He's got an amazing body, yeah? That T-shirt he was wearing today was painted on, and he's got that dark-haired, bad-boy brooding look. It's pretty appealing."

"He's a frat boy jock!" Paul gaped at him. Paul was an intellectual snob, and jocks had no place in his world except as objects of derision. For the typical reason, of course: the high school athletic teams' natural prey was the weak, intelligent queer boy.

"Makes him that much better to look at. Did you check out those muscles? Brad has a nice set of arms on him. And, man, you should see the view from behind." For just a second, Paul might have looked interested, but he squelched it with a contemptuously curled lip. Really, Sebastian was enjoying messing with Paul too much. It wasn't nice.

Not that he was going to stop.

"He could be playing you!"

"What, like flashing his well-formed pecs at me to get what he wants? Showing me his corded neck so I'll overlook his plagiarized paper?" Sebastian laughed. "He's straight!" He was pretty sure. "Even if it occurred to him to do it, he'd never be able to make himself." He grinned over at Paul, enjoying his flustered outrage openly.

"He could be trying to inveigle you!" Paul was so worked up he stood and leaned across his desk, planting his hands on the surface. "Get you obsessed with him, then get you to change his grade."

"You *cannot* be for real." Sebastian laughed more. "You think he's trying to trap me with his masculine wiles, yeah? Even if he is, do you really think I would be susceptible?"

Paul pointed a finger at him. "Mock me all you want, but I'm telling you, you need to keep an eye on Frat Boy."

"Oh, I will. I'll be watching Frat Boy very closely."

Paul glared at Sebastian and stalked out of the room, muttering something about coffee and traitors.

Sebastian chuckled to himself as he picked up the next essay from the stack he was grading. Paul was so easy to fuck with. Sebastian was probably going to have to apologize for it, but it had been fun while it lasted.

Truth was, Sebastian had kind of needed that. Just a little bit of stress release. For some reason, he'd been horribly disappointed when he'd seen Brad's paper this week. When he started reading it, his chest had felt like it was filling up with concrete. He was so mad he didn't even feel that amused disappointment he usually did when he caught a cheater.

He'd tried to shrug it off. Didn't work so well. He'd ended up taking a walk. Normally he'd contact a student outside of class for something like that, but he'd just wanted it over with. So he'd gone back home and gotten Brad's paper, scribbled the note on it, and went to Ari's class to deliver it.

Then he'd spent the rest of the morning rethinking all the crap he'd already let himself think about Brad. Maybe Brad was exactly what he looked like. Sometimes stereotypes fit.

But sitting in that coffee shop, having Brad apologize, felt like such a relief he'd had to smile. For a few seconds he'd almost let himself start a conversation.

Fuck, he had to stop this. He thought about that kid too much.

Maybe Toby wanted to troll the bars, check out some guys tonight. That would probably do the trick.

Sophie called that night. "I think I'm in love."

Sebastian smiled into the phone at his sister. "What've I told you about that love thing? It's just a word straight guys use to get girls into bed."

Sophie sighed. She didn't go for her usual line, though. "You don't really believe that."

"Eh." Verbal shrug. Sebastian pulled another plate out of the dish rack and started wiping it dry.

"You're just asking for it. You know that, right?"

Screwing one's face up in confusion made it hard to hold a phone between one's shoulder and cheek. He needed one of those dumb headsets, because Sophie had a knack for calling when he didn't have any free hands. "Asking for what?"

"Asking for Cupid to come and shoot you in the ass with one of his arrows."

"Then what, I'll fall in love with my own ass? Already happened. It's a lovely ass. Well-formed. And you know it's not Cupid—"

"It's Eros," she finished for him in a drone. Then she sighed, "Okay, so let's get the inquisition over with."

"What inquisition would that be, dear sister?" He asked, the epitome of surprised innocence.

Sophie snorted. "Puh-lease, just ask me about school."

"Oh, you want to tell me about your studies? Lovely, go right ahead."

"It's fine. It's the beginning of the semester. I like my classes. I took a few of the ones you *suggested*. Are we done?"

He put up with her talking about relationships, so she could put up with him talking about her education. Someone had to; Dad wasn't. "How few of the ones I *suggested*?" he asked pointedly.

She sighed so loudly he winced. "Three, okay? History of Women in Art, Anthropology, and I continued French." She said French as if it was a disease.

"French is a beautiful language," Sebastian said. Then he pulled out his trump card. "Someday, you'll have a lover who whispers French in your ear and you'll know if he's complimenting you or talking about food."

"Well, there is that . . ." She sounded more interested. "On that note, maybe it's time we started discussing relationships. Yours."

Done with the dishes, Sebastian leaned against the counter and let her start. Sophie believed talking about guys was one of the main benefits of having a gay brother.

"So, who do you have your sights set on now?"

"Nobody."

"Nobody? Please."

He smiled to himself but kept it out of his voice. "Nobody in particular."

"There's *noooo*body out there you've been eyeing and whose person you've been making designs upon."

"Hmmm. You sound skeptical." He drawled it. That always annoyed the shit out of her.

"Sebastian." Sophie's teeth were clenched. He could hear it. He smiled wider and snapped the air with the wet dish towel.

"Eyeing? Yeah. Designs on their person? No."

"What? Why not?"

Sebastian shrugged, almost losing the phone again. He caught it and said, "He's straight."

Sophie was momentarily speechless. *Score.*

"Huh. That's unlike you." True. "Are you *sure* he's straight?"

"Mmmm. Eighty percent sure, say."

"All right. We can work with that twenty percent. Tell me about him."

Sebastian shrugged again, grabbing the phone first this time. He was going to make her work for it. "He's cute."

"Like, fluffy-baby-animal cute or I-wouldn't-kick-him-out-of-bed cute?" She was getting that impatient edge to her voice again. Teeth clenching would commence any second. Sebastian smiled and started twirling the towel.

"Kinda both, actually. He's cute."

"Shit, this is useless." He didn't believe her. She never gave up that easily. "But I refuse to give up. Tell me about the sexy-cute part."

Sebastian rolled his eyes. "Beautiful muscles, and he's got these high, prominent cheekbones, almost Native American looking, yeah? And blue eyes. With a darker ring around the iris. Am I done now?"

Sophie heaved a sigh. "Just tell me what makes him baby-animal cute." He hesitated too long, and she pounced. "A-ha! Now we're getting somewhere. Talk."

Shit. "He's, I don't know. Macho, yeah? But I don't think he really is, I think it's an act."

"That makes him baby-animal cute?"

"Yeah." Sebastian had to clear his throat. "It kinda makes him seem vulnerable."

He could hear Sophie breathing. "Oh my God," she whispered. "You're in love."

Sebastian burst out laughing, then mocked her for most of the rest of the conversation, like a good older brother should.

Little sisters were annoying. After he got off the phone with her, the "love" thing stuck in his head long after he'd finished in the kitchen and wandered into his bedroom to study. He stared at the page of Herodotus he'd been trying to read. He wasn't so much translating from the ancient Greek as thinking about modern love.

Presumably he was capable of falling in love, right? He was twenty-eight, and he hadn't really had a serious boyfriend. No one had ever caught his interest that way. What if the reason they hadn't was because he could only fall in love with straight guys?

He realized he'd actually sat up straight at that thought. Jesus, he was losing it. That was just asinine.

He settled back against the headboard and shook it off.

Love. Riiiiight.

Besides, look at their father. Maybe Sebastian wasn't capable of falling in love at all.

Or worse, maybe—again, like their father—Sebastian was only capable of falling in love once, with someone who was totally wrong. Like, destroy-his-life wrong. Like, have-kids-with-him-then-run-off-with-his-coke-dealer wrong.

Shit, he'd sat up again. *Shut up.* This was worse than telling ghost stories around a campfire. Was he going to have to sleep with the light on? Fuck, he hated the aftermath of talking to Sophie.

Chapter 8

This wasn't a good feeling. Brad tried to figure out what the feeling was, lying on his bed, a sick lump floating under his ribs somewhere. If it had a color, it would be pea green and light brown. A big, crawling, swirling chunk of it. It felt like fungus or something, growing on something rotten.

He'd never cheated. Okay, well, he'd never plagiarized. A whole paper. It was more than just losing his scholarship that stopped him. It was the thought of what his mom and dad would say. Especially his dad. He closed his eyes, scrunching them up. His dad would kill him. His dad was always harping on not "misrepresenting" yourself. Plagiarism probably qualified as misrepresentation.

Brad groaned out loud when he thought of what his sisters would say. Especially Val. She already rode his ass for being a "player" and acting like a "stupid jock."

Easy for her to say. She got an academic scholarship. Val was starting next fall at State, where Ellie had gone to school. Intelligent sisters were some kind of curse. Even Olivia, who was only ten, was smarter than him.

The feeling floated up again under his breastbone, demanding his attention. Ugh. He wished he knew something that would make it go away. Maybe if Sebastian punished him.

Brad couldn't get his jeans open or his hand around his cock fast enough. He gripped it almost too tight and started pulling fast and hard. Imagining Sebastian watching him. Ordering him onto his knees. Reaching out and tracing his lips with a finger, then slipping it into Brad's mouth for him to suck on.

That was as far as Brad got before he was coming in his boxers. He curled up and rolled onto his side, the muscles in his ass throbbing. His balls emptied into his hand and all over his undershorts, and he groaned it all out. Fastest orgasm on record. He kept his eyes closed, and could see Sebastian's lips moving and hear his voice saying, *Good boy*.

Chapter 9

By the end of winter term, Brad figured Sebastian had forgotten he was alive. At least it looked that way to Brad. He'd turned the damn paper in—his last of the term—and Sebastian had taken it with a "Hmmm, thanks. I'll let you know if there's a problem." Then he'd shut his office door in Brad's face. That was the last time Sebastian had even looked at him.

The only consolation was that Brad got a B-. Once again, Sebastian didn't even look at him when Brad went up to get it at the end of class.

The guys at the frat were getting weirder, too. Especially Collin. No one bought his theory that Brad was gay, and they were giving Collin a raft of shit over it. But he kept hanging around Brad more and more. He used to only lift weights with them once a week or so, but now he did it all three days, and he'd started running with them the other days.

Theta Alpha Gamma wasn't exactly the sports frat. It was the second-string sports frat. TAG was a local frat, at Calapooya College only, and they didn't have a lot of money. But they did have one of those cool old-style frat houses, although it wasn't in the best of shape, and they handed out scholarship money. Which was why Brad was in it. It covered his dues and living expenses, as well as some tuition. He never could have paid for the first-string sports frat.

Collin had never been much into the daily frat group workouts until the last couple weeks. Now he was always around, and he was always, *always* taking his shower when Brad did. Fucker bent over in front of him every time, too.

Brad was pretty sure Collin was trying to trap him. Wave his hot ass in Brad's face until he sprung a boner to prove he was gay. Not that springing a boner in the shower was any kind of proof.

Shit. It was just one more thing to make Brad's life a little more stressful. By spring break, he was *so* ready to hole up at his parents' house.

He spent most of his break sleeping 'til noon, getting up while his parents were still at work and Max and Olivia were still at school, and spending some quality time in front of the computer with his dick in his hand. Then he'd make something for dinner so his mom wouldn't have to cook, and let everyone rave about how good it was while they ate it.

It went a long way toward making him feel better.

Until he got up Thursday at 10:30—he was planning on making a batch of his special Bolognese sauce and putting it in the freezer—and found his dad still there. "Hey, Dad. You said you had to work every day this week." Something about the way his dad was looking at him and not reading the paper made Brad uneasy.

Dad was sitting at the little round Formica kitchen table in the little yellow kitchen, looking at him very seriously, coffee mug cradled between his hands. "I called in sick," he said in his uber-calm voice.

Uber-calm was bad. Brad tended to associate it with disciplinary action. He swallowed. It'd be nice if he had something on besides boxers. "What'd I do?"

"You forgot to clean out your history cache yesterday." Dad was looking calmly at him.

Brad tried to work up some outrage. And some saliva. "You were snooping in my browsing history?"

For the first time, Dad looked uncomfortable. "Not until you threw your used towel in the hamper."

"Dad!"

"Brad, I've wondered if you were gay for years."

Brad's jaw dropped. He had to lock his knees to keep from falling over. "No, you didn't," he croaked. He stared at his dad a minute longer, but no, it still made no sense.

He needed coffee for this. Brad stumbled over to the coffeemaker and the cupboard full of mugs above it. He could feel Dad watching him the whole time he was pouring out the coffee—shit, his hand was shaking—and then the milk. Brad took a deep breath, grabbed his mug in both hands, and turned around to lean against the counter. "I only figured it out last month. How could you know if I didn't?"

"Your high school football coach called me when you were fourteen and told me to 'keep an eye on your deviant tendencies.' That man was a homophobic jackass. I told him you were what you were and if I found out he was giving you any shit, the least he'd have on his hands was a discrimination charge."

Brad's extremities went numb. He barely kept from losing his coffee mug. "So that made you think I was, uh, gay?"

"Let's just say it was the nail in the coffin." His dad nodded at him, arms folded across his chest, and tipped his chair back. Like they were discussing sports.

"I don't . . ." Brad stopped and cleared his throat. "You already thought that, uh . . . ?"

"Little things. I can't even tell you what they were anymore. Maybe your mother remembers better if you need to know."

Fuck. "Mom knows?"

Dad nodded calmly and held out his mug. Brad looked at it blankly. What was he supposed to do with that? "So, who else thought I might be?"

Dad stood up and walked to the coffeemaker. "I don't think anyone else thought you were. Not with the way you slept around in high school. And, I assume, in college?" He quirked an eyebrow. Brad swallowed. "So, are you really gay, or bisexual?"

Stupidly, Brad wondered where his dad had learned a word like bisexual. The things they put on TV these days. He shook his head slowly. He'd thought about this. Practiced saying it to himself after his talk with Ashley. "I'm pretty sure I'm gay."

Cool, he hadn't stuttered at all.

Dad leaned against the counter next to him, sipping his coffee. "What about all those girls?"

Brad took a sip of his own coffee. Some kind of fortification. "I think what I was with them was drunk and stupid and faking it."

"So you've really known all this time?"

Brad shrugged, feeling more and more comfortable. He took another sip of coffee. "More like I knew something wasn't right, I think. I guess I knew, kinda; I just didn't think it could be true. Like it was a mistake and some day it would go away. It just . . . didn't." He sucked in a breath, his chest loosening up a little more. "You know, denial."

His dad clapped him on the shoulder. The encouragement pat. "Well, when your mother gets here, we can all talk about it together. We'll help you through this."

"Mom? I thought she had to work . . ." Of course his father had called his mother and she was on her way home. What was that going to be like? Was she upset? "Did you *tell* her you thought I might be gay?" That was all he needed, his mom forewarned and forearmed.

"No, she already thought so. We've talked about it, so I called her . . . Why are you looking at me like that? It's not like someone died. You're just gay. You just be who you are and the rest will work out fine."

His mom had texted Val and Ellie before she left work.

"When did you learn how to text?" Brad was starting to get over "dazed"; the way his family was acting, he was approaching annoyed. Not that he could explain why, exactly.

"Val taught me. In case of emergencies."

"Me being gay was an emergency?"

"No, sweetie! No! It's a celebration. When Val gets here—"

Brad exploded. "Why are you guys taking this so well?"

Dad finally looked up from the paper he was reading at the table. "Would you rather we took it badly?"

"No! Just . . . shouldn't you be upset? Adjusting? *Something*? What about the grandchildren you won't have to carry on the family name?"

His mom shrugged. "Not my family name. I don't care."

His dad went back to his paper, saying absently, "Don't worry, even if Max turns up gay too, I'm sure Val will manage to get herself pregnant without the benefit of a husband." Mom halfheartedly whacked Dad in the back of the head. He ignored it. Brad stared at them. Dad was back to reading the paper, and his mother was rattling around in the cupboards, going on about some sirloin tip roast she'd been saving for "an occasion."

"Gah!" he finally yelled, and stomped off to the guest room to slam the door. He heard his mother ask his father faintly, "What was that all about?"

He didn't hear if his dad bothered to answer.

Brad couldn't explain why he was disgruntled with his family's easy acceptance. Maybe he needed them to have a hard time with it so he'd have a reason not to come out all over the place.

Not as if he didn't have enough reason, anyway. He could barely say the word, especially when he was talking about himself. So yeah. Made sense that he wanted to wait to unveil his hard-on for guys in general. He was still adjusting.

Didn't make his siblings any less annoying. Except Max and Olivia. Max was disgusted, but in a non-offensive way Brad could understand. Kind of the way he'd been disgusted at fourteen when he'd figured out he was supposed to want to touch girly parts.

Olivia just shrugged. Apparently ten-year-old girls weren't interested in gay guys.

Unlike nineteen- and twenty-five-year-old girls. Val and Ellie were excited about it. They started asking him dumbass questions about guys and clothes. "You two are such fucking stereotypes," Brad said. Mom hit him half-heartedly in the back of the head. He ignored it.

Ellie somehow managed to make him go out with her and Val after dinner. He mostly grumbled at them and pouted in the backseat. She took them to a place the next town over so they could talk without running into anyone they knew.

Ellie sighed when Val ordered a drink and then produced her nice, shiny, fake ID when the waiter asked for it. "Mom probably thinks I'm going to stop you from doing shit like that when you come with me, huh?"

Val shrugged. "Nah. Probably not."

"That's a relief."

The night turned into a drunken love-fest. The familial kind. "'M gonna have to call Dad to come'n pick us up!" Ellie announced joyfully after killing off the second pitcher of beer.

It was good, though, because they finally fucking *listened* to what Brad had to say. "I dunno," he shrugged drunkenly. "I had that football coach, you know? Coach Radcliffe?"

"Yeah," Ellie sighed. "He was *hot*."

Brad nodded solemnly. "Yes. Yes, he was. Smokin' hot. He used to shower with us sometimes, y'know?"

"*Real*—ly?" Ellie was sounding kinda squealy.

Val clapped her hands together in delight. "Our brother is talking about cute guys with us!"

Brad scowled at her. "He was just, like, everything I wanted to be, y'know?" Val and Ellie nodded raptly. "I guess he was kinda everything I wanted. So one day he's showering with us, and I'm watching him. Not, like, *looking* at him, just sorta out of the corner of my eye. There were these mirrors, y'know? Near the showers? 'N' if I was in the right spot and he was in the right spot, I could watch him in the mirror. I thought he never noticed, y'know?"

More nodding, with a little bit of horrified delight thrown in. Brad snorted at them before going on. "I was watching him, and I glanced up and he was looking at me in the mirror. Right into my eyes. So my heart, like, stops, then it starts banging away and I don't know what I think's gonna happen, but I managed to keep it under control, y'know? S'not easy for a fourteen-year-old guy to do that. But he's looking in my eyes and I start to chub up—"

"Eeeewww!" Val squealed, closing her eyes and plugging her ears. "Ican'thearyouIcan'thearyouIcan'thearyou," she chanted, drawing the attention of the people at neighboring tables. Ellie knocked Val in the back of the head, shutting her up and dislodging her hands. They shared a mutual scowl.

Yeah, okay, that might have been a little graphic to share with his sisters. "Sorry, my bad," he muttered.

"Whatevs, go on," Ellie commanded.

Brad took a deep breath. "So he calls me into his office after that, and he starts talking about 'fags' and how jocks who were, uh, gay never made it anywhere and no one liked them and, I dunno, a bunch of shit. Said he expected all his 'men'—that's what he called the guys on the team, y'know, men—said he expected us all to show a healthy interest in girls. He scared the shit outta me. I don't even know what all he said, but . . ." Brad trailed off and shrugged.

"So that's why you were in denial?" Val asked after a short silence.

"I dunno. I think I mighta been anyway." More shrugging. "I mean, 'member? I was almost six feet when I was fourteen and everyone was always tellin' me I was a jock 'n' macho 'n' shit. I just din't know, y'know?"

Now they looked confused. And bleary. Beery. "Din't know what?" Val asked.

"What I *was*. I mean, I kin'a thought I might like guys, but it was like ever'one tellin' me I liked girls . . . so I did, I guess. Least, I tried."

Ellie had that little wrinkle between her eyebrows. "But, I mean, y'just forgot 'bout the whole lusting-after-your-coach thingy?"

"No, I just . . ." Brad heaved out a sigh and took a sip of beer. "I thought maybe it was just one a'those things, y'know? Like I's just confused."

"Oh, Brad," Ellie said softly, looking remarkably sober all of a sudden.

Brad shrugged.

The next morning, after their parents and Max and Olivia had left, the three of them lay around groaning. Especially Brad, who'd gotten into Val's cigarettes the night before. In general, hangovers were par for the course, but the nicotine headache: ugh. "Does Mom know you smoke?" he asked Val from the depths of his coffee mug at around 2 p.m.

Her shrug was a little pained. "Probably," she rasped. "Don't worry, I'm sure it's just a phase."

Snorting hurt his head.

Chapter 10

H is first Saturday night back at school. Another fucking party. Yee. Haw.

One he had to at least make an appearance at. TAG had a weird rush system—they had a long selection process over spring term and then the pledges had to live in the house for summer term. Most of the pledges' initiation rituals revolved around fixing leaky pipes and repairing various holes in the drywall. It was basically free labor.

The first Saturday of the term was their first rush party of the selection. The rest would be more formal, but this one was raucous. Lots of girls, lots of beer, lots of other stuff.

Brad wasn't drinking, though. He hadn't been doing much besides moping lately. He was short on sleep, food, and beer. He was also bored as shit, holding up a wall, wishing he could disappear into his room. Not that it was much of a haven anymore; Kyle had emailed him over spring break to tell him the frat wanted to move another guy into their room. They couldn't really say no. Brad should have known it would be Collin. Murphy's law. But it wasn't until he got back to school on Sunday night that he found out.

Collin, who was trying to out him. Brad sent Collin a narrow-eyed glance across the living room. Some chick was talking him up, but Brad caught Collin staring at him. Collin looked away quickly. Brad watched him a moment longer, but Collin was avoiding his eyes. Brad sighed and turned away. To see a group of girls looking at him and talking.

Brad rolled his eyes and thought about what Ellie and Val had said. They (so kindly) agreed with him on his looks—he wasn't model-worthy by quite a bit (although they kept going on about his cheekbones for some reason). According to his loving, kind, and brutally honest sisters, most of his appeal was in reputation and disinterest. He was disinterested; girls chased him. If they caught him (or could make it look like they did), they got a little "street cred," and it made other girls want him.

"It's a vicious cycle," Val had intoned seriously.

Made absolutely no fucking sense to him. He ignored the girl-gaggle and let his eyes wander around the room. Stoned guy, drunk guy vomiting out a window, drunk girls in a pack, girl with no shirt, Kyle leading girl upstairs, drunk guy, Sebastian, guy propping up wall next to Sebastian, guy with a bong, guy jerking and seizing to music, girl dancing next to him with a horrified expression—

Wait. Sebastian?

Brad's heart started running around in his chest like a frightened rodent. He squinted through the low light, but it wasn't really *that* low. It *was* Sebastian.

Ah, shit. What should he do? *What would Ellie tell you to do?* Dammit, why was he thinking about his sister at a time like this?

Because she gave great advice. Sometimes. Who else did he have to ask? For some reason the thought of asking Ashley flitted through his mind. Yeeeeah. That was gonna happen. In another lifetime. Ellie it was.

Brad dug around in his front pocket, refusing to look away from Sebastian as he pulled out his phone. He couldn't lose him.

At party, he texted to Ellie. *He's HERE! What do I do?*

What? U rly need me to tell you? Talk to him, dumbass.

What do I say?

Thx for not turning me in to prof for plagiarism.

That's it?

Sure u can handle it from there.

No. Can't.

Yes.

No, please?

Turning off phone.

Bitch.

How come she wanted to tell him every little thought she'd ever had about him being gay, but she wouldn't help him when he asked?

Okay. He could do this. How hard was it? He'd watched tons of girls try to pick him up over the years. He'd just do what they did, right?

Somehow that didn't seem quite kosher, but Sebastian started moving toward the door. Brad followed before he could stop himself or think anymore.

Chapter 11

"Hey! Sebastian!" Sebastian heard the voice behind him once he was a good hundred yards from the frat, heading toward the closest campus parking lot. It was dark with a little mist drifting up off the ground, swirling around the tall firs that surrounded the college. Sebastian was almost to the halo of lights that marked the campus boundary. On-campus it was well-lit. Off-campus, one lonely streetlight was sputtering away a block back.

For a split second, Sebastian felt like he was in a ghost story. He shook off the prickles up his back and turned. It was probably a kid from history class.

The shouter was only ten feet from him before he managed to believe what his eyes were telling him. "Brad."

"Hey." Brad stopped and stood a couple feet in front of Sebastian, shoving his hands in his pockets. He looked nervous.

Silence. Sounds of the party in the distance. A car starting in the campus lot. For some twisted reason, it made Sebastian want to smile that Brad was mildly freaked out. He'd always been inappropriately amused by others' discomfort. Especially guys who wouldn't stop popping up in his head too often. Usually naked.

He probably shouldn't, but he let Brad fidget with his hands in his pockets for a few seconds before breaking the silence. "Did you want something?" At least he was trying to smother the smile.

"Yeah. Um, I just saw you in the party and I wanted to say thanks."

"For coming to the party?"

Interesting. Brad was blushing. "Um, no," he kind of laughed at himself, glancing up at Sebastian. "For not turning me in for plagiarizing that paper." Brad cleared his throat. One of his hands snuck out of his pocket and started scratching behind his ear. He shoved it back in.

"No problem. Everyone gets to screw up, once." Although damn he'd been annoyed when Brad had.

Brad nodded and looked around again. His hands fidgeted in his pockets, trapped.

Sebastian took pity on him, finally. "So, you belong to Theta Alpha Gamma, huh?"

"Yep." Brad nodded, looking grateful, and rushed on. "Kinda surprised to see you there."

"Yeah?"

Brad looked less sure again. Then he opened his mouth and shocked the hell out of Sebastian. "That guy you came with, are you, um . . . is he gay?"

Sebastian's eyebrows shot up. "Why? Are you interested in him? If you want to know anything about him, you're going to have to ask Toby yourself." Well, that was just . . . annoying.

"What?" Brad's eyes got big. "No." Brad forced another laugh. Not really believable. "I was just wondering if, you know, you guys were together."

Sebastian laughed. "Oh. No, we aren't together. I don't do the boyfriend thing, much. I'd hardly leave him all alone at a frat party if we were seeing each other. What kind of boyfriend would that make me?" Sebastian smiled. "Can't even claim to be much of a friend, leaving a gay boy all by himself at a frat party."

Brad started to reach up to scratch behind his ear again, but stilled his hand abruptly. He shoved both hands back into his pockets and took a deep breath. "So, uh, that History of Rome class, huh?"

"Yeah. It's a class."

"Yeah. It's kinda kicking my ass. I mean, I know it's only the first week of the term, but . . ."

"I was kind of surprised to see you in it this quarter. It didn't seem like you were into the previous section much."

Brad couldn't quite meet Sebastian's eyes. He mumbled something about his schedule and scratched his ear again. Suddenly he took a deep breath and looked back up at Sebastian. "Um, I was hoping maybe you could help me. Tutor me or something?" He caught himself scratching behind his ear again and dropped his hand.

Sebastian cocked his head. "I probably shouldn't, since I'm the TA." And because, in spite of all the reasons he'd given himself not to be, he was still attracted to Brad. But . . . "Yeah, sure. We can do that sometime. I'm free Wednesday evening—"

"Like, maybe now?" Brad asked, his voice overly loud.

Sebastian eyebrows went up again. Did Brad have any clue what this was beginning to sound like? "It's Friday night." Brad flinched but held his gaze. If Sebastian didn't know better, he'd think Brad was coming on to him. In a cute, juvenile, inept way. If he didn't have a clue, Sebastian should probably give him one. If he did have a clue, Sebastian would be giving him an opening. "Why Brad, if I didn't know any better, I'd think you were trying to get me alone and take advantage of me."

Brad choked on air.

Okay, Frat Boy *was* gay. Or bi. Or bi-curious. At least, judging by the way he was sucking air like a fish on dry land. Sebastian was willing to admit to a healthy interest in the answer; Brad did a little something extra for his libido.

Sebastian eyed him for a few seconds, watching him get even jumpier. Just when he judged Brad was about to flee screaming into the night, Sebastian asked, "Are you a tourist?"

"Uh . . ." Brad was a little wild-eyed.

"Just taking a walk on the wild side. Wanna see how the other half lives. Curious."

Brad looked down at the ground and scratched furiously behind that ear, then pulled on the lobe. Sebastian was beginning to fear for his skin back there. "I'm sort of more serious than that," Brad finally said. He flicked a look at Sebastian from under his brows and then was back to watching the ground.

Sebastian's impatience—and his libido—got the best of him. After waiting for Brad to look at him for a few dozen silent seconds, he bent forward to put himself in Brad's line of sight. Brad startled a little. "How serious?"

Brad took a deep breath and held it a second. "I'm gay." It sounded like he'd used all that air he'd taken in to push that out. "I haven't been with . . . a lot of guys. I'm, um, attracted to you, you know?" Brad straightened his shoulders as he spoke, finding some courage somewhere, or bravado. "Really attracted to you."

"Ah." Sebastian cocked his head. "So, I guess the only question left is, are you top, bottom, or verse?"

"Verse?" Brad snapped his mouth shut, looking embarrassed at how naive he sounded.

Sebastian wasn't so sure continuing this was such a great idea, but . . . "Versatile. Or maybe you don't do anal?"

Brad's mouth moved a few times, like he was trying to say something but couldn't quite shove it out. Just when Sebastian figured it wasn't going to happen, Brad blurted, "I want you to fuck me."

Well, that was a nut-tightener for you.

He just had to figure out what to do with Brad. Oh, his body had some ideas. It was already shuffling blood around, sending adrenaline through him. He tried to approach this logically, but his rational mind was getting drowned out by the blood rushing in his head. Shouted down by the part of him that just *wanted.* The part that had wanted Brad for a while.

Brad wanted him too, right? He was clearly inexperienced, but it wasn't like Sebastian was, or like he'd hurt Brad. Sebastian wasn't going to take advantage of him. He just wanted (*oh yeah, he wanted*) to give Brad what he'd asked for.

"Come home with me?" Sebastian's mouth was moving before his rational mind was completely on board, but it was fighting a losing battle. It was trying to tell him something, but he doubted it was important right now, anyway. He could always listen later.

Chapter 12

Brad was nervous. As. Hell. Like, his-stomach-was-eating-his-liver kind of nervous. He should have had a beer at the party, then maybe he'd loosen up some. Which he probably needed to do since he'd just offered his virgin ass to Sebastian.

Oh God. What if Sebastian had a huge dick? Like, beer-can thick? He'd seen a couple like that on the internet. Just the sight of a dick that big would make him clench up tighter than a nun. He slouched down even farther in the passenger seat of Sebastian's car, looking out the window. His brain reminded him he'd been preparing himself for *this*. Getting fucked. He could feel his face blazing. Thank God Sebastian couldn't see it in the dark.

God, he hoped Sebastian wasn't some kind of mind reader. Given the choice between mind reader and beer-can dick, he'd take mind reader, though.

Sebastian's hand on his thigh made him jump. It felt kinda nice, warm and heavy, but Brad was feeling jumpy, he guessed. He figured he had the right to some nerves.

"You really haven't done this much, huh?"

Brad cleared his throat a couple of times. "No," he croaked.

"We don't have to. I can take you back, or we can just go somewhere and talk."

Brad cleared his throat again, and an important thought finally filtered through the adrenaline haze. "Why are you doing this?"

He could feel Sebastian looking at him, but he just stared out the windshield. "Taking you home with me? Hoping you really meant it when you said you wanted me to fuck you?"

Oh God. "Yeah. That." Brad slouched down lower. Was he terrified or more excited than he'd ever been in his life? He couldn't decide.

Sebastian pulled into the parking lot of an apartment complex. One of those ones built out of cardboard in the last ten years, with about five hundred units in it and lots of open, concrete-riser stairways. He didn't say anything, just parked the car, taking his hand off of Brad's thigh to maneuver the steering wheel. He stopped the engine and turned to Brad. "Hey." His voice was soft. "Look at me."

Brad did it without conscious thought. Sebastian told him to, so he did. He swallowed as he looked at Sebastian looking at him. What did he see? Sebastian had unbuckled his seatbelt and leaned back against the window, one leg up on the bench seat. Brad couldn't see him that well because the light was behind Sebastian, but he knew what he looked like from memory. He was so, just, *cute*. Sexy. His face was square, and his nose was long with an arch. He had a strong jaw and wide, large eyes with black lashes, and Brad could barely look at his mouth without getting hard. Speaking of which . . .

"You're hot. Not just your body, which you have to know is amazing. I really want to see you naked. I like looking at you, and yeah, I've been checking you out. I don't really know you, but I like what I do know."

"Even with the whole, you know, cheating thing?"

Sebastian smiled, light bouncing off the corner of his upturned lips. He pulled himself away from the door and started leaning forward. "Yeah. You didn't lie, and you didn't get pissed and act like you had the right to do it. You didn't try to tell me it was really your paper but you'd been selling it to other people on the internet for years and only now needed to use it for yourself."

Brad swallowed. If he had to guess, he'd say his heart picked up another beat per minute for every inch closer Sebastian got. "Someone tried to tell you that?"

Sebastian's smile grew, or maybe Brad could just see it better. "Yeah. People try to tell me it's a coincidence, too. Somehow they wrote a paper that's the exact same, verbatim, as one floating around on the web."

Sebastian's lips were maybe ten inches from Brad's. He could smell cold night air and underneath it something warm and maybe a little spicy. Not cologne; just Sebastian. Brad's breath hitched in his chest. "I bought it because I wanted to impress you."

Sebastian stopped moving forward, and his eyes widened. He looked . . . delighted. "You bought a paper so I'd notice you?"

Fuck, Brad just was a loud-mouthed idiot, wasn't he? He nodded. "Guess you noticed me, huh?"

Sebastian leaned forward the rest of the way. "I'd already noticed you." He laid his mouth on Brad's. He didn't kiss; he brushed their lips together until Brad came forward that extra millimeter and kissed Sebastian. He cupped the back of Brad's head and tilted it, sliding his tongue over Brad's lips and into his mouth, and then Brad didn't really remember much clearly except finger-tingling, heart-pounding want.

Sebastian pulled Brad forward, bringing Brad's chest against his. Brad had handfuls of Sebastian's coat and the desire to get to what was underneath, but he couldn't concentrate on anything because Sebastian's tongue was stroking inside his mouth and his hand was on Brad's head, directing him, fingers scrubbing through his short hair.

Suddenly a horn blared, really close, and Brad shot up. His heart ricocheted around in his chest and he looked wildly out the window. He felt Sebastian's fingers on his cheek. "It was you, Brad."

"Huh?" He couldn't see anyone outside.

"You hit the steering wheel and honked the horn."

It took a few seconds to sink in. Brad looked down at Sebastian uncomprehendingly. He could see him better here in the light coming from the window. Sebastian had that teasing smile on his face. That, more than his words, told Brad everything was okay. His muscles relaxed and he collapsed against Sebastian, his forehead in the crook of Sebastian's neck.

"Let's go inside, yeah?" Sebastian said into his ear, his breath making Brad shiver. Brad nodded into Sebastian's neck.

Sebastian led Brad to a second floor apartment, walking silently beside him, and somehow it made Brad feel . . . he didn't know, exactly. *Protected* wasn't quite right, but it wasn't all wrong. He felt like Sebastian was sort of taking care of him. Solicitous. Walking through the door after Sebastian had opened it and stood aside, Brad felt Sebastian's hand brush his lower back. Guiding him or something.

Inside the apartment, Sebastian took off his coat and threw it over a chair, walking into the kitchen area while Brad shucked the light jacket he'd managed to grab on his way out of the frat. It was dark and silent in the apartment. Sebastian turned on a light over the stove, making it just bright enough that Brad felt comfortable.

"Want something to drink?" Sebastian asked, staring into the open fridge. He was gripping the handle really hard.

"No. Um, no thanks. I just kinda want to . . . can you come here?" Brad wasn't having any second thoughts, but he needed to get this show on the road. He scratched behind his ear but made himself stop.

Sebastian slammed the fridge shut and walked into the living area and right into Brad, lifting his head to Brad's, stroking Brad's side with a soothing hand. Brad opened for him immediately, following Sebastian's lead when Sebastian kissed him. Let Sebastian pull him down onto the couch, then lay on his back when Sebastian pushed on his shoulders.

Sebastian propped himself on one elbow over Brad, distracting him with kisses for he didn't know how long. At some point he felt Sebastian's hand slipping under his shirt, Sebastian's fingers feeling his muscles and dipping into Brad's navel. He shuddered when Sebastian did that, and gripped his shoulders. Sebastian pulled back from their kiss and whispered, "I'll be right back."

What? Where was he going? Sebastian leaned back in and kissed him again. "Right back," he promised.

Left to himself on the couch, Brad started to get nervous again. He'd forgotten it before, with Sebastian touching him and making him feel like a live wire. He sat up, unsure what he should be doing. Hesitantly, he pulled his T-shirt over his head. When it cleared his eyes, Sebastian was standing in front of him, something in his hand, staring at Brad.

Sebastian dropped the lube and condoms he was carrying onto the coffee table in front of the couch, focused on Brad's chest. Brad couldn't look away from the lube and condoms. *Three* condoms? He swallowed, thinking of Sebastian's fingers covered in lube and touching him. Pushing inside him and stretching him open.

Then Sebastian was shoving the coffee table out of the way and getting on his knees in front of Brad, and Brad's heart went into triple time. A whimper escaped him when he felt Sebastian's tongue lick around his nipple, making it tingle and tighten up, then sealed his lips around it and sucked.

"Oh. Sebastian, that's—fuck." Brad grabbed Sebastian's head, holding it to his chest.

He couldn't seem to control his body anymore. He was arching into Sebastian and gripping his head and his biceps, small, high-pitched noises escaping him without permission. Sebastian licked and kissed and sucked his chest while Brad shook and hung on.

Sebastian pulled him off the couch and onto the floor next to the coffee table. Brad let him undo his jeans and pull them down, straining and trembling in his hands as Sebastian explored his abdominal muscles. Making noises that he should probably be trying to squelch when Sebastian's tongue licked around his navel. He was gripping Sebastian's head so hard it had to hurt, but his fingers weren't responding to the logical part of his brain.

When Sebastian sat back on his haunches to pull off Brad's shoes, Brad ran his hands down his own ribs and into his boxer-briefs and wiggled out of them frantically while Sebastian unbuttoned his jeans. Brad's cock, trapped under his waistband, bounced free when he wiggled his boxers to mid-thigh. He felt Sebastian watching it bob around and his dick got harder and tighter. Too tight for his skin.

Eyes still on Brad, Sebastian shoved his pants down. Brad swallowed. Sebastian's cock was pushing out, making a huge bulge in his black underwear. He pulled them down, his cock slapping him in the stomach and leaving a smear below his navel. Brad stared at that wet spot a few seconds before he could make himself focus on Sebastian's hard prick.

"Thank God," Brad said under his breath. Sebastian wasn't huge. He was big, but not scary. Much. He was also beautiful, dark with blood, and Brad wanted to feel that shiny mushroom head with his fingers.

Before he could reach for it, Sebastian stretched his naked body across Brad's and groaned.

Oh. Oh fuck. Skin everywhere against his and pressure on his cock and even smooth, hot skin pressed up alongside it. Sebastian's cock. He thrust when Brad moaned and arched up, hands digging into Sebastian's back. Brad's dick lined up perfectly next to Sebastian's, and he slid them together, using his hips and Brad's movements to build a rhythm.

Brad felt everything: Sebastian hard against him and that scratchy-soft hair and the rubbing friction and even the sweat on Sebastian's abdomen, and it dragged a noise out of him he'd never heard before. One of those noises that came entirely from the gut.

Sebastian kissed him, opening him wide and shoving his tongue in and stroking inside Brad's mouth, and he felt like Sebastian was inhaling the noises he was making. He got lost in what was happening, until Sebastian pushed one of his legs up to his stomach. Brad grabbed it and yanked it up higher. Opening himself for Sebastian.

That was when the panic hit. Just a little, but it died down when Sebastian looked into his eyes and ran a lubed-up finger behind Brad's balls. Then he was making those noises again, but a lot more of them. Sebastian was on his knees and one hand, crouched over Brad circling his opening with one finger, fucking Brad's mouth with his tongue.

When Sebastian pushed gently against Brad's hole—a lot more carefully than Brad had been with himself—and his finger slid in, Brad gasped, tearing his mouth away from Sebastian's, staring at him. Yeah, it burned a little, but he'd done it to himself enough to be prepared for that. Fuck, he ached for more of it, knowing it was Sebastian inside him. The stretch felt good. Skin—someone else's skin—felt a hell of a lot better than plastic. He sucked in breaths and watched Sebastian watch him while he eased himself in farther. Then he was kissing Brad again, rhythmically moving one finger, then two. Sebastian found his prostate and he jerked with the sensation. Moaning into Sebastian's mouth.

Sebastian stopped when he was fucking Brad with three fingers and Brad's noises were coming closer together and louder and he was pushing onto Sebastian's hand because he needed just a little bit more, a little bit farther in.

Sebastian didn't ease out of the kiss; he ripped himself away. He looked as dazed as Brad felt. Fingers still in Brad, he tore the condom package with his teeth and put it on one-handed, slicking himself up while twisting the fingers of his other hand inside Brad, lighting him up. Brad sucked in a sharp breath, eyes fixed on Sebastian as he brought his hips between Brad's thighs.

Everything slowed down from frantic and desperate to slow and intense. Sebastian eased his fingers out of Brad, guided himself to Brad's ass. Brad sucked in another breath and held it, hands gripping Sebastian, staring into his eyes as Sebastian slowly pushed inside him. The smooth head pressed against his hole, working its way in easily at first, but then his ass clamped down and it fucking hurt. Brad took a deep breath as Sebastian pushed slowly but insistently, and he felt the muscle relax, Sebastian's head pushing in. The pain started to melt away.

Then Sebastian suddenly stopped, looking surprised. Staring down at Brad.

Chapter 13

I t was after he'd shoved past the inner muscle, just his head inside Brad, that it hit Sebastian what a complete fucking idiot he was. His blood pounded in his eardrums and he fought his instinct to push in farther, no matter how welcoming and hot and perfect Brad felt. Brad was wide-eyed, shaking, gripping Sebastian's biceps like he couldn't decide whether to push him away or pull him closer, and Sebastian finally realized. He stopped easing himself inside Brad and stilled, hanging over him.

The whole night with Brad replayed itself in fast-forward in his mind: Brad popping his head up like a scared rodent when he'd accidentally hit the car horn. Being sure that if he turned on all the lights Brad would freak out, so only turning on the low light in the kitchen. Scrabbling through his nightstand for lube and condoms, trying to get back to Brad before Brad panicked and bolted. The look in Brad's eyes when Sebastian pushed his leg up to his stomach.

"I'm your first, aren't I?" Sebastian looked down at Brad, eyes wide, dark hair spiky with sweat. He looked terrified and elated. Breathing heavily through his mouth. He swallowed, hard, his Adam's apple bobbing, pressed his lips together and nodded quickly. Then he just stared at Sebastian.

That look nearly undid him. Brad was trusting him to make this good. Looking like he was relying on Sebastian to initiate him into some whole secret world he was desperate to be a part of. Like he'd been pressing his nose up against the toy store window for years and now he'd finally gotten that shiny red die-cast fire truck with the working ladder.

"I wish you'd told me." If he had known, he might not have taken Brad's virginity at all, or at least not this way, but they were already here. He had to make it as good as he could now. That idea made his heart pound even harder and pulled at his nuts. The whole fucking thought of being Brad's first—the first guy inside him—was making him lightheaded.

Brad swallowed and gripped Sebastian tighter, looking truly scared for the first time that night. "If I'd told you, would you still have done it?"

"I don't know." But that was a lie. He would have done it.

Brad suddenly dropped his head and shoulders back on the floor. He'd been tensed and curled up toward Sebastian, but now he was relaxed, letting things be what they were. The look in his eyes was raw. "I wanted it to be you."

He looked so vulnerable and exposed. Sebastian felt something moving in his chest. A little thing tugging itself toward Brad. It wasn't as if Sebastian was going to stop now—he *couldn't* stop—but looking at Brad's face made him feel like maybe this whole thing was somehow right.

Carefully, Sebastian moved. He pressed slowly deeper into Brad. Brad's eyelids dropped and then fluttered back open, eyes looking for Sebastian. Sebastian moved again, pulling out and pushing gently back in with short strokes. Not slow or fast. Careful. Working his way deeper. Trying to read Brad's face.

He stopped moving, fighting the pull to sink farther into Brad. "Feels good?" he asked quietly. He hung there in the darkened room, arms extended, holding himself up over Brad's body. Maybe trembling a little. He wanted to hear it.

Brad licked his lips, barely keeping his eyes open. "So good," he said. Out of breath. Sebastian smiled as Brad curled his upper body up toward him, and he gave Brad what he wanted, leaning down to kiss him.

It was possibly the sweetest kiss he'd ever shared. Especially with someone he was inside of. Short and strangely innocent, even when Brad's tongue slipped into his mouth and tentatively stroked his. Then he retreated, and Sebastian was left hanging over him still, looking into Brad's eyes.

Brad finally released his biceps and started playing with his hair, but then he pulled one hand back and stroked down to Sebastian's chest, watching with those wide, light eyes. He scraped his fingernails through the patch of rough-smooth hair between Sebastian's pecs. Giving Sebastian chills. Tentatively he touched Sebastian's nipple, and Sebastian murmured something encouraging so Brad wouldn't stop exploring. Brad watched his hands play on Sebastian, but Sebastian found himself watching Brad's discoveries play across his face.

As Brad explored, Sebastian began to move again, watching him fight his falling eyelids, listening to the catch in his throat every time Sebastian pulled out. Brad's fingers stilled and his eyelids fluttered shut, but he forced them open to watch Sebastian again.

Sebastian wanted to see him lose that fight.

"You're just like I imagined," Brad breathed. "You're beautiful."

He looked alarmed by what he'd blurted out, his gaze flying up to Sebastian's, mouth opening to say something. So Sebastian shoved himself into Brad harder and deeper than before. Balls deep, fighting his own eyelids. Brad arched up, moaning louder this time, mouth open, eyes closed, exposing his neck. Sebastian leaned down to run his lips up Brad's throat. "*You're* beautiful," he corrected.

Brad whimpered. Sebastian sucked skin into his mouth and nipped it, moving faster and harder. He brought his body down, pushing himself against Brad's skin, wanting as much as he could get.

"Oh, God, Sebastian. That. Fuck." Sebastian smiled into the skin under Brad's chin and kissed it, then let his tongue play. The wet head of Brad's cock was painting pre-cum on his stomach, Brad's hands trapped between them, gripping Sebastian's chest. He surged in harder, pushing a sharper sound out of Brad.

Sebastian's hips—and instincts—started to take over. He was fucking Brad more seriously now. Feeling it more. He dropped his head and concentrated on making Brad feel more, too, changing his angle.

"Oh fuck!" Brad arched up convulsively. "That. There. Again, Sebastian."

So he did. Again and again and again. Until Brad was writhing and whimpering. Completely lost. Sebastian lifted his head enough to watch Brad's face. He'd never had this kind of influence on anyone before, never made someone's body respond like this. Certainly never had someone's responses affect him so much. He almost thought he could come just from watching Brad come apart.

He really, really wanted to see that. He pushed himself up farther, propping himself on one arm, and worked a hand between them, grasping Brad's cock, thumb circling around the head.

Brad clutched at Sebastian's other wrist and curled up to him, eyes opening, watching Sebastian stroke him from under heavy lids. Brad's mouth hung open and he panted and moaned. It was the sexiest thing Sebastian had ever seen.

He stroked up on Brad's dick, twisting his hand, and Brad came undone, his fingernails sharp on Sebastian's wrist. He shouted, curling up off the floor, eyes closed and face screwed up tight. Brad pulsed in his hand and his ass clamped down on Sebastian's cock. He pushed into the resisting muscle hard and looked down to see cum all over Brad's stomach, and more leaking onto his fingers.

It was like watching the USS Enterprise take off at warp speed, when the stars started streaming by in long lines and you went from a standstill to faster than light. His own sensations suddenly overloaded and catapulted him into orgasm. He slammed into Brad, probably way too rough, but he wasn't really in control of that anymore. He came until he saw the stars streaming by, his whole body shivering with the sensation. Holding himself above Brad until he couldn't anymore and then collapsing onto him. Getting both of them sticky and probably crushing the guy.

Not that Brad seemed to be complaining. He was a big, strong jock. He could take Sebastian's weight for a minute or two.

One of Brad's hands landed clumsily on Sebastian's back and started moving up and down his spine. He felt Brad's breath stirring his hair, and propped himself up on Brad's chest to see him after a minute.

There was too much on his face. Sebastian couldn't even begin to figure out what all those emotions were. If he had to name them, fear and joy would be at the top of the list. Brad's eyes were shining and huge, the pale blue almost luminous in the light from the kitchen. His lips were dark and puffy from Sebastian's kisses.

He looked vulnerable. Fuck, that was sexy. Sebastian leaned forward and kissed him. Another achingly sweet one. Placing smaller kisses around his lips as he eased away. He could feel Brad shivering. "Cold?"

Brad shook his head, mute, just staring at him. He leaned forward and kissed Brad's chin this time. "Let me get something to clean you up. Stay here and I'll take care of you."

It took a minute to sink in, but then Brad nodded. His eyelids drifted shut over hazy eyes, but flew open as Sebastian eased himself out of Brad. Brad shivered, then sighed and let his eyes fall closed again.

In the bathroom, Sebastian threw away the condom while running the water to get it warm. He stood there watching it stream into the sink.

He'd figured out a long time ago that part of what got him off was how his partner reacted to him. He thought he was generally pretty good at reading them, their responses, figuring out their needs. But he'd ignored all the signs that Brad was completely inexperienced with men because he'd wanted to fuck him so badly. He'd royally fucked up tonight.

Maybe.

He was surprised to find out how much he liked Brad. He'd been with a lot of guys, but most of the time it was just sex. With Brad, he didn't know if it was the virginity thing or something deeper, but he wanted to maybe explore it some more. They could have a hell of a good time in bed for a while if Brad was interested.

But Brad was kind of like a frightened wild animal. The closeted frat jock. Timid without the pack; terrified when exploring outside his natural environment. Some public-television narrator started doing the voice-over in his head. *Liable to strike out when threatened with exposure.*

Maybe. Or maybe not. Sebastian sighed. He'd just have to leave it up to Brad. He grabbed a washcloth and reached for the now-steaming water. On the inside of his wrist were three little crescents: marks from Brad's fingernails breaking his skin. Sebastian dropped the washcloth in the running water, bracing himself on the counter with his arms. His stomach tightened up into a ball.

Fuck. He'd just taken Frat Boy's virginity.

Chapter 14

Everything looked different inside his head. Brad wasn't sure what it would look like if he opened his eyes. He was too tired to do that right now, anyway, so he let himself zone out a while. He floated, feeling so fucking good and, just, high.

So much better than he'd thought. Like he'd been having sex through plastic wrap his whole life and now he got to actually feel skin for the first time.

He startled a little at the touch of a warm washcloth on his stomach and Sebastian's weight next to his thigh. He smiled because it tickled when Sebastian wiped the cloth across his stomach, but he couldn't open his eyes.

Sebastian cleaned him up, and Brad shivered as the moisture on him cooled. Sebastian's lips were soft on his abdomen, beside his navel. A bolt of sensation shot down his gut to his dick, but it was kind of tired right now. Too tired to move.

"Brad," Sebastian breathed into his ear. "We need to relocate. My roommates could come home, and when they find naked men in the living room, they assume they're up for grabs."

Brad's eyes shot open. "You have roommates?"

Sebastian sounded amused. "Yeah, two. They won't show up anytime soon, but I don't want you passed out on the floor when they do."

"Oh. Uh, yeah. I don't want that much, either." Jeez, even his voice sounded different. Or maybe his ears heard things differently.

"You can come to bed with me, or I can take you home. My roommates won't tell anyone you stayed, but other people live in this complex that go to Calapooya."

Brad stared at the ceiling, frozen. He knew what he wanted, but it had nothing to do with other people from school seeing him leave Sebastian's apartment in the morning, and everything to do with needing to know what Sebastian wanted. Did he just want Brad to leave? Kinda like Brad wanted the girls he'd hooked up with to just leave?

Before he had to figure out a way to ask, Sebastian planted a hand on either side of Brad's shoulders and leaned forward until he was only inches from Brad's face. He had such a sexy grin. Playful. Brad caught himself before he sighed.

"If you stay, I'll wake you up early so you can make your escape. We can do other stuff you've never done with a guy before."

Brad's mouth dried out. Sebastian leaned down and kissed him. "I'll stay," he rasped when Sebastian pulled back.

Brad's horizons weren't broadened much more that night. He found he was dead tired. Once he stumbled into Sebastian's room—dark and hard to see, but there was the bed—and Sebastian had curled up behind him with an arm around his waist, he couldn't stay awake. It was kind of a relief, really, since he had a feeling it would be awkward.

Sebastian woke him just before dawn with a hand on his dick. Too bad he couldn't get an alarm clock that did that.

Or, even better, an alarm clock that stroked him slowly while thrusting against his lower back until they both came. Then kissed his neck and let him doze a few more minutes before waking him up with another warm, wet washcloth. Now *that* was a snooze alarm.

"You want me to give you a ride?" Sebastian kept his voice low, maybe because of the roommates, or maybe just because it seemed like the kind of time and place where speaking softly was right.

Brad stretched. He didn't feel awkward, just all warm and relaxed. Sated. He thought about it a few seconds, but, "No. I'd kinda like to walk. Guess I need to think."

Sebastian smiled and walked him to the door. He didn't say anything about seeing Brad again. Well, not "seeing" like the night before. He did kiss him at the door, though, and said, "See you in class on Thursday."

What was Brad supposed to say? *Not if I show up here before then.* Or maybe, *You don't want to fuck me again?* Or the classic, *Where do you see this relationship going?*

All the awkward came back in a rush. He shoved his hands into his pockets and said, "'Kay." He looked at Sebastian, who was watching him, then turned around and walked out the door.

He felt way less sated by the time he made it back to the frat. It was still pretty gray—the sun hadn't really popped over the horizon, yet—when the house suddenly loomed up in front of him. Brad didn't know if it had been hiding or if he'd just been thinking too hard, but there it was, like a big haunted house. He crept across the porch and opened the door cautiously, not exactly sure what he was being cautious about. Maybe a skeleton jumping out at him and yelling, "Fag!"

Instead, Julian was standing blearily in the entrance hall, blinking and swaying with a trash bag clutched in one hand and his grabber-thingy on a stick in the other. Julian was a bit of a neatnik. He probably hadn't even gone to bed, just drank all night and started cleaning when the last person passed out.

"Hey, Brad," he hiccuped.

"Hey, Jules." Brad moved on past him, breathing a sigh of relief that the first guy he ran into was still drunk and preoccupied with garbage.

In his room, it was just light enough to see that there were two people in Kyle's bed. Kyle had himself wrapped around some girl. She looked familiar, so Brad looked closer: Ashley.

Thank God she was moving on.

In his own bed were two girls he didn't recognize. Collin's bed hadn't been slept in. The thought of why two girls might want to wedge themselves together into his little single bed made him pause a second. *Whatever.* Fortunately, they were too hungover to complain much as he rousted them out and sent them on their way.

He dropped into bed in his shorts and a T-shirt, huddling under his blankets. He needed a shower, and he was fucking cold. He also had some aches left over from his night with Sebastian. Well, one significant ache.

He shivered a little, thinking about it. The ache was kind of nice. Like a souvenir. He pulled the blanket over his head and lay there, smelling sex and Sebastian.

Best Dutch oven ever.

Chapter 15

Brad didn't shower until Sunday evening. By then, Collin and Kyle were starting to bitch.

All weekend he'd been doing his normal shit, working out, inventorying the kitchen or doing homework, ignoring texts from his sisters demanding to know what had happened, not returning messages from his mom, and it would hit him. *Sebastian fucked me.*

Once Kyle snapped his fingers in Brad's face, looking annoyed. "Dude, you mad about me seeing Ashley or not?"

Not really. "I don't care."

"Good. Uh, I kinda think she's over you, man."

Brad shrugged. Kyle didn't even look at him weird.

When Brad finally saw Sebastian again on Thursday afternoon, he choked. He'd been thinking about Sebastian all week, thinking what he wanted to do with him (naked), how he wanted to tell him he'd like to see him again. A date, maybe? Should he ask him out? Were gay dates the same as straight dates? Maybe on gay dates you got to see better movies. With, like, action and shit.

Oh, fuck. Sebastian would want to see an art film or something. He might turn Brad on something fierce with the intellect shtick and those glasses, but that didn't extend to seeing movies in black and white where the entire thing was just two people talking to each other.

No movies, then.

Of course, maybe with Sebastian he could try that thing he'd always wanted to try. Where you cut a hole in the bottom of the popcorn bucket and stuck your dick in it, then waited for your date's fingers to find it.

Nah. That probably didn't show a lot of class.

What Brad *hadn't* been thinking about was how Sebastian hadn't made any move to see him again, or even shown interest in it. He'd just let Brad walk out his front door and that was it. Brad wasn't in the student directory, so Sebastian couldn't call, but he knew where Brad lived. He knew what class Brad would be in on Tuesday morning.

When Sebastian walked into History 203 a half hour before it ended on Thursday and looked directly at Brad, Brad's stomach nearly gave up its breakfast. Sebastian had a pretty serious look on his face, and not the look he usually had, where it seemed like he was kinda amused with the world in general.

Shit. What'd that mean? And damn it, now he had something caught in his throat. It felt like a giant hairball. He looked down, away from Sebastian. He was afraid to look at him. It wasn't like he was any good at reading people's emotions, but he didn't want to take the chance that this would be one time he managed it.

Every time he forgot and looked over at Sebastian, it seemed like Sebastian was watching him. Ashley, who was sitting between him and Kyle for some unknown reason, startled him by hissing in his ear. "Did you sleep with him?"

Brad choked and coughed. He threw a wild look past Ashley to Kyle. Ashley rolled her eyes. "Like he's gonna care," she whispered. "So, did you do him?"

Because Brad wasn't with it, he answered. "He sorta did me."

Ashley looked impressed. Brad snuck another look at Sebastian. He still looked serious. Brad jerked his eyes to the table in front of him instead.

"So you're gay?" Ashley breathed.

"Oh yeah. I'm gay."

Chapter 16

S ebastian thought maybe the sex was just like a temporary high. The intensity with Brad was maybe like getting drunk—great at the time, but the hangover made it not worth it.

When he tried to explain that to Sophie Wednesday night, she told him he was a hopeless case.

"Case of what?" Sebastian asked.

Sophie didn't answer. Instead, she tried to find out more about Brad.

"He put a lot of trust in me, yeah? He chose me, for some reason." Sebastian got up from the table where he'd been studying and wandered into the living room.

"Maybe he likes you."

He had a feeling they weren't talking about Brad liking his skills in bed. "Where did I go wrong? Everything's a relationship with you, yeah? I don't think so. He didn't say anything about that." He flopped on the couch and slouched into the cushions.

She snorted. "Yeah. Because guys are always talking about their feelings first, then the sex. So, are you going to let him choose you again?"

"Mmm, yeah. It's not like I'm getting nothing out of it. He's hot. I'm attracted to him. I want to mentor him." Wanted to mentor him all over.

"Uh-huh. His gay sex mentor?"

Sebastian smiled to himself and put his feet up on the coffee table. Paul hated when he did that. "Yeah. Like, in ancient Greece, a guy in his twenties would mentor a teenaged boy. The older guy was the *erastes* and the younger guy was his *eromenos*. I'm Brad's *erastes*."

She snorted. "Did you have one of these sexual mentors to introduce you to the gay lifestyle?"

"I was a special case."

"Uh-huh. Of course you were. Did any of your friends have one of these 'mentors'?" She'd learned that verbal quotes thing from him. He was a good mentor.

"Well, yeah. Most guys I know started out with a boyfriend, and screwed around with him until they got their sea legs."

"Ah-ha! So, you're going to be Brad's boyfriend!"

Sebastian laughed at her until he fell over on the couch, then once he had the breath, he mocked her for the rest of the conversation.

He finally got it straight in his own head, even if he couldn't seem to make Sophie understand. He needed to make sure that Brad was okay with what happened. Offer more if Brad was interested in exploring it, because Sebastian was. Brad needed to know he was desirable, right? He might be sort of fragile now. A good *erastes* wooed his *eromenos*.

Chapter 17

The situation with Brad was a delicate thing, a guy discovering his gay tendencies when he lived the last of the staunchly heterosexual lifestyles. Sebastian felt a "wait and see" approach might be best before he began the wooing in earnest. His poor, naïve (well, that was arguable) *eromenos* might be bashful. Unsure.

So Sebastian gave him time to adjust. Stretch his mind around what had happened. He'd been hoping Brad would pop up somewhere, well-adjusted. Drop by his office or his apartment, ready to continue his mentoring sessions.

Which didn't happen. Every night when he closed his eyes, he could see Brad lying under him, and by Thursday morning he needed to find out what Brad was thinking. He definitely wanted Brad again, even without the mentoring.

To his surprise, his stomach was a little achy before he walked into Ari's class. That was different. Of course, he'd never been a mentor before.

Brad wouldn't look at him. He looked scared and uncomfortable and possibly mortified. Sebastian closed his eyes, sitting back behind the desk. Guilt washed over him while he waited for class to end so he could take in next week's papers and supervise handing back this week's.

He'd fucked Frat Boy and now Frat Boy was freaking out. Yeah, Brad had said he wanted it and acted like he wanted it, but Sebastian had enough experience that he should have known something was off. He should have spent some time talking to Brad rather than letting the dick-tator run the show.

He'd really, really wanted Brad. Had fantasized idly more than once about what he might look like without any clothes on.

Brad was beautiful naked.

Sebastian could appreciate all types of men. He loved soft skin as well as textured, and muscles were nice but so was leanness. As a connoisseur of men, bears and beer guts had their place as readily as soft, nubile twinks.

Brad was smooth, almost hairless, and he had beautiful muscles. Not insanely huge ones, but solid and defined. And Sebastian really needed to stop thinking about what Brad had looked like that night, sitting on the couch, pulling his T-shirt over his head, then looking at Sebastian in that scared, vulnerable, hopeful way. Sebastian was beginning to suspect Brad might have ruined him for anything but jocks.

Sebastian opened his eyes and Brad was watching him again. This time Brad's ears went red and his eyes widened before he jerked them away.

Oh, hell. He was going to have to make sure he hadn't scarred Frat Boy for life.

It took for-freaking-ever for Ari to wind up, and when class was finally over and people were filing past Sebastian's desk to turn in and/or pick up papers, he was relieved to see Brad in the throng. He kept an eye on him surreptitiously.

Right before Brad and his friend Kyle made it to the desk, Brad said something quietly in Kyle's ear and, when Kyle nodded, turned and walked away.

Sebastian didn't even think about it. He grabbed Kyle and planted him behind the desk. "Make sure no one takes a paper that isn't theirs, put the new ones in a stack and take them to the History Department receptionist," he hissed into Kyle's ear, then grabbed his backpack and took off after Brad.

He caught him outside Miller Hall. It was misting and gray, but he could make out Brad pretty easily even though it was one of those Pacific Northwest days when you weren't sure there actually was a sun. Recognized the set of his shoulders. He didn't call out to him, because he had a feeling that would freak Brad out. Instead, he just sped up until he was walking next to him.

Brad took a small misstep. Sebastian slowed down a little. He glanced at Brad, who was looking at the ground, still walking. "Come to my office with me so we can talk." He could actually hear Brad swallow as they walked along, but he gave a jerky nod. Sebastian exhaled with relief.

He managed to keep his mouth shut until they were almost to his office. "Just because you had sex with a guy doesn't mean you're gay," he murmured softly.

Brad stopped dead. He stared straight ahead, jaw clenched. "I *am* gay," he said quietly but distinctly through his teeth.

He sounded pretty convincing. "Okay, sorry," Sebastian said. They stood there for a minute, Sebastian looking at the side of Brad's face while Brad stared down the deserted hall. "Brad, look at me."

He swallowed, but he turned his head enough to see Sebastian. He met Sebastian's eyes briefly, then his gaze flickered away.

"I'm sorry if I pushed you last weekend or anything, yeah?"

Brad looked at him in confusion, meeting his eyes again. "Pushed me?"

Well, this was uncomfortable. "I'm sorry if I talked you into more than you were ready for."

Now Brad stared at him like he was certifiable. "I asked you to fuck me." His voice was just a little loud, and he flinched and glanced around nervously before turning back to Sebastian. "I thought *I* talked *you* into it." Judging by the color in his face and the way his eyes dropped, that was just a little more than Brad meant to say.

Sebastian suddenly felt like himself again. "So, you were thinking I felt, what? Used?" He let himself smile slightly at Brad.

Brad's mouth twitched, but he didn't look up. "Yeah."

Sebastian took a small step closer to Brad. "I didn't feel used. And you didn't feel used?"

Brad's eyes flickered up again. It was amazing how Brad was actually a few inches taller but Sebastian still felt like Brad was looking up at him. "No. I didn't feel used. I wanted it."

Sebastian let his voice drop until he was nearly whispering. "You think you might want it again? With me?"

Brad's eyes widened. He flushed, but nodded. It occurred to Sebastian that the flush might not be embarrassment; maybe it was arousal. "You still coming with me to my office?"

"Yeah." Brad's pupils were dilated, and his voice husky. Sebastian smiled at him and turned to lead the way.

The short hallway to the 232 offices was about fifteen feet from where they stood. When Sebastian turned into it, he heard voices coming from his office. *Fuck.* Probably Paul and Michelle. He stopped walking, and Brad crashed into him. Just that little contact made his whole body buzz, and he reached for the door handle of the supply closet they were standing beside. He wrenched it open and dragged Brad inside with a hand wrapped into the front of his shirt.

Inside, with the door closed, it was completely dark with just a strip of dim light leaking in around the door. Sebastian debated turning on the light, caught up in the mechanics of getting them off and getting them out, but Brad reached for him, grabbing his attention and yanking on his coat. Like a kid who who'd found some rare, delicious treat in the checkout line at the store and would lie on the floor kicking and screaming to get it.

Sebastian was happy to be Brad's candy. Maybe it was the way he yanked the hair on the back of Brad's head, but Brad opened right up for him as soon as their lips met.

It took approximately five seconds of pacifying Brad's frenzied tongue for Sebastian to realize what he'd done. He'd awakened an addict. One of those rare, special guys who—once he figured out he wanted boys—*needed* it. The big it.

Brad was a gift any *erastes* would give thanks on his knees for. Later, when he wasn't busy. A good *erastes* met his *eromenos'* needs, first and foremost. What Brad needed now was someone to indulge him. Assuage his ache. Sebastian was *so* up to that job.

He planted his hands on Brad's waist and aimed him toward the only bare strip of wall he could remember in the place. Brad let him walk him backward, hands in Sebastian's hair, sucking in air through his nose and stroking Sebastian's tongue in his mouth. Stumbling over Sebastian's feet and his own.

When Brad hit the wall, he grunted then pulled Sebastian in tighter, twisting against him. Brad's eagerness was starting to rub off—literally—on Sebastian. He pulled away enough to say, "Spread your legs," against Brad's open mouth. Brad did it immediately, making room for Sebastian and bringing them closer to the right height. Sebastian stepped into him, grinding against him, making him gasp into his mouth.

Sebastian wanted to take his time, but they were in a supply closet. He slid his hands around from Brad's back to start working on his fly, unbuttoning his jeans, slipping a hand inside to cup him through his boxer-briefs while unzipping him with the other hand.

He felt the hard shaft and promised himself one day he'd see it in the light.

Brad's kiss got more frantic when Sebastian palmed his dick, fingers searching for his balls. He started making those noises Sebastian had liked so much the other night. Mewling. Sebastian pushed against Brad's mouth harder, controlling it with his tongue, reaching for his own fly. He yanked his jeans open and shoved them and his shorts down far enough to get his dick out. Then he ground it against Brad's hard cock, still covered by his briefs.

Sebastian pulled out of the kiss, lips wet from Brad, feeling Brad panting into his face. He dragged his dick slowly back and forth over the hard ridge of Brad's erection, and Brad whimpered some more and started to reach for his shorts, but Sebastian grabbed his wrists and pinned them against the wall.

He wasn't usually quite this domineering, but it seemed right with Brad. Brad obviously liked it. He could have pushed Sebastian away anytime and taken control himself simply through superior muscle, but he let Sebastian hold him against the wall and torture him, shuddering and twisting and making those noises for him.

The thought of all that strength under his control made Sebastian even hotter. He nipped Brad's lip lightly with his teeth. "You wanna feel my naked cock rubbing up against yours?" he whispered.

Brad nodded frantically. "Please."

Well fuck, how could he refuse such a polite request? He let go of one of Brad's wrists and reached down to shove his hand inside Brad's briefs.

Chapter 18

Brad thought he was going out of his mind. Sebastian's hand was exploring him, fingers searching out all his landmarks and sensitive spots, tickling his balls, even squirming in between his thighs and his scrotum, reaching behind to feel the swollen base of his dick. He still felt the heat from Sebastian's erection on the other side of the fabric trapping him, and he wanted that against him so much he reached down with the hand Sebastian had freed just to feel it.

Hot, clammy skin against his palm, Sebastian thrusting into his hand, cockhead slipping through the circle of his thumb and forefinger. Brad groaned.

Sebastian stopped and pulled away. "Shhh. You can't make too much noise, there're people in my office, honey."

Something about what Sebastian had said caught his attention for a second, but he was going to have to think about that in more detail later. He nodded and bit his lip. Sebastian licked along where his teeth dug into his skin. It wasn't really helping with the noise thing.

"Do you think you can be quiet? If you can, I'll take you out of these briefs."

"Please."

"Tell me you can be quiet, Bradley."

"I'll be quiet."

Sebastian let go of Brad's other wrist and brought that hand down, too. He moved back, creating a pocket of air between them, and carefully pulled the waistband of Brad's briefs out and around his dick, tucking it beneath his balls. Then he took Brad's hand off his cock and pushed up against him.

Brad couldn't stop the noise he made when he felt Sebastian's dick against his. It must not have been too loud, because Sebastian wasn't saying anything, just wrapping his fingers around both of them, holding them together, circling Brad's head with his thumb. Brad thrust into the sensation, and Sebastian let him.

Sebastian's hand held them tightly together, the skin of his fingers slightly rough. The skin of Sebastian's cock, though . . . Fuck. Brad let his head fall against the wall and just let his hips run the show. Soft and silky and hot and getting slippery. Making him vibrate. Static electricity.

Sebastian didn't move much; he let Brad thrust against him. Which was good, since Brad was losing control. Mindlessly fucking in and out of Sebastian's hand, thin skin against thin skin, blood pounding underneath and he felt so fucking *safe*. His hand was so strong, like he could hold Brad all day if that's what Brad needed him to do. Brad's fingers dug into Sebastian's back and his hips moved faster. Trying to generate a current.

Sebastian's other hand came up, fingers digging into the back of Brad's skull, pulling him down. Sebastian's mouth by his ear, whispering, "Do what you need, hon. Make it feel good. Anything you want. So good." On and on and on, urging Brad to go faster. Tightening his fingers until Brad was pulling on his shoulders, using him for leverage to thrust his dick through that tight grip.

Then all of a sudden he was there, a bolt arcing from Sebastian's nuts to his, igniting him, and then Sebastian's mouth was over his, trying to muffle the noises he couldn't stop himself from making. His legs locked up. He was pumping everything out into Sebastian's hand. Sebastian stroking him through it when he couldn't move, hot liquid silk from Sebastian, groaning out how good Brad was through his own orgasm.

Then panting and jelly knees and Sebastian cupping his face, one hand sticky. "Come over to my place and have dinner with me Saturday night."

Brad kissed him. Played in his mouth. Saying "thank you" and "yes" that way because he was too fucked out for words.

Sebastian seemed to understand.

When Brad pulled away, he managed to ask, "Like a date?"

"Yeah. Like a date."

Chapter 19

Michelle was laughing her ass off and Paul was glaring and muttering by the time Sebastian was cleaned up enough—and his legs were steady enough—to make it to the office. Thank God there was a sink in the closet. Although he still had a nice, big wet spot on his shirt. So did Brad, and he'd seemed considerably less steady on his legs. But they'd managed to look semi-normal by the time they'd stumbled out of the supply closet.

Not that it mattered, because when Brad came he'd made so much noise they'd probably heard him over in Miller Hall.

"What's that for?" Michelle asked.

"Huh?" Was she talking to him?

"That stupid grin you have on your face."

"Oh." He felt it stretching his mouth wider as he dropped his backpack on the floor next to his chair and collapsed into it with a satisfied sigh.

Paul was still glaring. Michelle had started laughing again. Finally she sputtered, "Is the grin because you just fucked someone Paul calls 'Frat Boy' in the supply closet?"

Seriously, the grin had better give up soon, because his cheek muscles were starting to hurt. "Nope."

Michelle's sputtering laughter died down and she measured him with her eyes. "Ahhh. Did you just have sexual relations with 'Frat Boy' in the supply closet?"

"That's confidential information." Too bad he couldn't stop smiling.

Michelle winked at him. "I see."

Paul's mutterings finally exploded out of him: "I told you, you needed to keep an eye on that jock!"

Sebastian made his face as serious as possible. "Paul, I want you to be assured that I have been keeping a lot more than my eye on Frat Boy."

Michelle laughed so hard she nearly fell out of her chair, tears leaking from her eyes. Over her laughter, Sebastian told Paul, "I need the apartment to myself Saturday evening, yeah?"

"If you think I'm going to clear out of my own home so you can invite some fucking jock over and—"

"I'll give you the number of that guy I met at the Slaughterhouse last month. The cute twink with the ass like a juicy apple."

Paul struggled, the whole battle written on his face. Juicy-apple-ass won. "Fine," he spat, then stood and stormed out of the room. Sebastian smiled over at a tear-stained Michelle and picked up his extension to call Toby. Chances were he already had plans (not involving their place, please), but he wouldn't be as hard to finagle as Paul anyway.

God bless juicy-apple-ass.

Chapter 20

"**N**eed some help?" Collin's voice behind Brad in the shower startled him out of his fantasy. The one where he was in the shower with Sebastian tomorrow night, Sebastian's hands on him, smoothing soap over his ass, licking water droplets off his collarbone. His dick hard and insistent against Brad's thigh.

Oh, fuck. He had a boner. Not the sort of half-hard thing he might get after working out, but the full-on curl-up-and-kiss-the-abs kind. Frantically, he looked around the shower room.

Collin was the only guy there. Suddenly, Brad was pissed. So mad, steam was coming off him. Or it would have been if the shower weren't already steaming hot. He rounded on Collin—showering at the nozzle next to Brad, as usual. He could take him, boner or not.

"Dude, I've had enough of your shit. You aren't going to convince anyone I'm gay. There's not even anyone here to see your little act, so can it." He ended up with his index finger an inch from the guy's nose, pissed and breathing heavy and still so fucking turned on.

Collin stared at him in incomprehension. Then his eyes cleared and he leaned forward. "Is that what you think I've been doing?" he murmured just before he sucked Brad's finger into his mouth. Looking into his eyes the whole time.

Collin had beautiful eyes, light hazel and almond-shaped and looking like he wore eyeliner. He swirled his tongue around Brad's finger and hollowed his cheeks. As if Brad's finger was the best thing he'd had in his mouth in, like, ever.

Oh, fuck. Warm and wet and soft and better than the inside of any girl. Brad stared, wide-eyed and frozen. Collin pulled his mouth off of Brad's finger with a pop, and Brad's breath made a little hitching noise in his chest.

Brad cleared his throat a couple of times while Collin looked at him, eyes heavy-lidded. "You aren't trying to trap me?"

"I'm trying to trap this," Collin said, reaching out and wrapping his hand around Brad's cock. His eyes slowly traced down Brad's body, until he got to where his hand was squeezing Brad's shaft.

Collin licked his lower lip, pulling on it with his tongue. Slicking it up with saliva.

"Oh, fuck," Brad choked.

Collin looked back into Brad's eyes and dropped to his knees.

"Oh, God, dude. I can't—" Brad's voice got stuck in his throat when Collin's tongue reappeared, licking almost delicately into Brad's slit. Collin stared into his eyes and Brad watched the water sluicing down his shoulders. Felt the stinging pellets hit his own lower back, and somehow it made him more sensitive to the mouth on his dick.

"You taste good." Collin dropped his eyes and started licking Brad like a lollipop. God, his tongue was just fucking obscene and so, so hot and wet and pink and fuck, what was that word? Agile.

Brad planted a hand on the wall to keep himself upright. He was trying to work up to stopping Collin, but wasn't sure he could.

"There's no one here but us," Collin whispered right before he sucked the head of Brad's cock into his mouth, tonguing the ridge and stroking up the underside to his head, swirling around it.

"Uh." Brad's higher brain shorted out. What was he gonna do, pull his dick out of the guy's mouth? It would take a stronger man than him to do that.

Collin sucked him down his throat without warning, and Brad yelped. Before he really knew how they got there, Collin had one hand on Brad's butt cheek, urging him to fuck his mouth, one hand on his own dick, and he was blowing Brad's mind. Looking into his eyes.

They were too light; hazel, not brown.

Brad shut his eyes. Fuck, he'd never ... no girl had ever made him feel like this giving him a blowjob. Their hands weren't that strong or maybe it was the occasional scrape of stubble or the sheer suction power. Or just because it was a guy. Brad didn't know and didn't particularly care.

Collin swallowed on him again, and Brad felt the cum right there, boiling over. He couldn't even warn Collin, but Collin didn't seem to care as those muscles behind Brad's balls contracted and expanded and shot down Collin's throat.

Collin was moaning around his dick, and when he could, Brad looked down to see Collin coming into his own hand as he licked

Brad clean. Brad was panting hard, leaning heavily on the wall, so loose he felt like gelatin on a skeleton.

Thank God I don't have to suck him now.

Because he'd never done it, and he might suck at it (haha), but mostly because he wanted to be on his knees in a shower with Sebastian, tasting Sebastian's cum in his mouth.

Fuck. Sebastian.

Brad collapsed back against the wall, pulling his dick out of Collin's mouth before Collin seemed totally ready to relinquish it. Collin had licked him all clean, but Brad didn't feel so clean inside. Some internal organ beneath his ribs was trying to turn itself inside out or something.

Collin stood up after a minute and shut off the water. The showers had been running the whole time. Val would kill him if she knew he'd been so wasteful.

Why the fuck was he thinking about her right now? *Because she'd call you a loser for what you just did with Collin.*

"Sorry," Collin said. Brad looked at him in confusion. "I should have asked if you had something going with someone first, huh?" He looked ashamed, maybe, and sad. Humiliated?

Brad cleared his throat. "What makes you think . . . ?"

"You called me Sebastian."

Brad closed his eyes and leaned his head against the tiles. "Fuck."

"S'okay man. My bad. Hard to turn down a blowjob. I won't say anything."

He could feel his face flaming. "I'm not really . . . he's not really. We just hooked up a couple of times."

"So you're not exclusive?"

Brad's eyes popped open at the hopeful note in Collin's voice. Collin was watching him intently.

"I don't know if we're anything." He hated the way his voice came out. It sounded sad, the same way Collin's had a few seconds before.

Collin looked at the tile wall and traced some grout with a finger. "Oh. I get it." He took a deep breath and nodded his head once, as if agreeing on something with the wall. Then he looked at Brad again, turning his whole body to face him. "I'm really into you, Brad. Like, this could be more than a random shower hook-up, if you wanted. So, um . . ." He laughed shortly, not really sounding amused. "If you ever figure out what you have with Sebastian and it's not, um . . ." He ran a hand through his dark hair.

"What I want?"

"Yeah," Collin said softly, back to talking to the wall. "I'd try, you know. To give you what you want."

Brad wasn't the best at following emotional subtext, but he was pretty sure he was getting what Collin was saying. He leaned toward Collin and kissed him on the cheek.

"Okay." At Collin's suddenly hopeful look, Brad thought maybe he needed to explain that a little. "If what I have with Sebastian doesn't work out or turn into anything, we can see what happens with you and me."

"Oh." Collin looked back at the wall, smiling sadly at it.

Brad cleared his throat. "Um, sorry." He should probably get the hell out of here and give Collin some time alone. He pushed away from the wall, but stopped after two steps. "Thanks." Was that what he should do? Thank the guy for the blowjob? He was uncomfortable as hell, and he was sure Collin knew, but he couldn't just walk away and say nothing.

"Anytime." Collin's voice didn't sound right, but Brad had used up his emotional subtext allotment for the day. So he sighed and walked out. Brad thought about watching Collin come at his feet, moaning around Brad's cock, and felt even worse.

He scrubbed off his dick in a sink.

Chapter 21

Brad went straight over to Sebastian's. He didn't know if Sebastian had classes Friday or what, but was hoping he would be home. It was barely nine.

Sebastian answered the door. "Hey!" he said, sounding pleased rather than the annoyed Brad was afraid he'd be. He let Brad in, scratching his head and yawning. He had on pajama bottoms. Only.

When Brad saw Sebastian's roommate on the couch, he stuffed his hands in his pockets and tried not to look at the way Sebastian's chest hair made that beautiful dark line down the center of his torso.

The roommate—Brad thought it was that guy Sebastian had come to the frat party with, Toby maybe?—gave a long-suffering sigh and looked at Sebastian. "I suppose it's time for me to leave for class, huh?"

Sebastian just smiled at his roommate, a toothy grin. Brad stood there, uncomfortable, while the guy grabbed his backpack and left. Right before he walked out the door, Brad heard him mutter something about "frat boy."

He cleared his throat, staring at the floor. After another few seconds of silence, Sebastian said, "Hey," again, but it was softer now. He walked over to stand in front of Brad, circling the side of Brad's neck with his hand.

Brad looked at Sebastian. He was totally fucking this up. He'd planned on being all cool and maybe never mentioning the whole Collin-cock-sucking thing, seeing where things went with Sebastian. He didn't even know how he'd ended up here. When girls had come to him wanting more, he'd hated it, partly for how pathetic it was— didn't they have more self-respect than that?—and partly because of how shitty it made him feel.

He almost turned and walked out. But Sebastian stroked a thumb across his jaw once and asked, "Is something wrong?"

"Collin sucked me off in the shower." It just tumbled out of his mouth.

Sebastian blinked, his head jerking back slightly. His thumb stopped that soothing stroke, but he didn't move his hand. "Okaaaay," Sebastian finally said. "And you're telling me this because . . .?"

Oh God. Brad was just another piece of ass for Sebastian. "I almost stopped him."

"Why?" Sebastian's short laugh sounded just a little weird. Weird enough that Brad kept talking.

"Because of you."

Sebastian dropped his head and blew out a breath. His hand tightened a little on Brad's neck. He looked back up into Brad's eyes. "Okay."

They looked at each other.

"Okay?"

"Okay, as in 'Okay, tell me why because of me.'"

"Because if someone other than me sucked you off I'd break his jaw."

Sebastian looked at him, his eyes dancing across Brad's face. "We never said this was anything exclusive," he said slowly. "We never said this was anything."

Oh, God. Sebastian *had* been with someone else. Not that Brad had any room to complain, because they'd only been together twice, and the first time was supposed to be a one-off. Not to mention the whole Collin-in-the-shower scene. "I know."

Sebastian's eyebrows drew together. "Do you want it to be exclusive?"

Brad swallowed the glue in his mouth. "Yeah."

"You just let some guy suck you off in the shower." Sebastian's hand slid down from Brad's neck to rest on his shoulder.

"I know," Brad whispered. He closed his eyes and hung his head. "He's one of my roommates."

Sebastian dropped his hand from Brad's shoulder. *Fuck.* "Brad, look at me." His voice was so strong Brad's head snapped up before he realized what he was doing. Sebastian had a funny look on his face. "Have you ever had *any* guy suck you?"

Sebastian had to know the answer to that one. Brad shook his head.

A little smile flirted with the corners of Sebastian's mouth. "And you didn't ask him for it, right?"

Brad's heart started to knock lightly on his ribs. He swallowed. "No, he just . . . I was thinking of being in the shower with you and I got, you know." Deep breath. "I got hard and he was there and the next thing I knew he was on his knees. I mean, I was going to step away, but he *licked* me."

How sick was it that telling Sebastian about it, looking into his eyes, was getting Brad excited again? Now Sebastian had that slightly teasing smile on his face. It was really wrong what that smile did to his insides. Shouldn't he feel mocked instead of turned on?

Sebastian stepped forward and got in Brad's space, eyes just below his, slipping one hand around the back of his neck and gripping Brad's hip with the other, wide-legged stance bracketing him. "And if I give you what you want, tell you I'll make this exclusive—for now—you won't do it again, will you, Bradley? It'll just be me."

That fast, Brad was mostly hard again. He wanted to grab Sebastian and bury his face in the crook of his neck, grind his hips into him. He left his hands in his pockets. "Just you," he croaked.

Sebastian slowly lost the smile and lifted both hands to Brad's face, tracing his cheekbones with his thumbs. He looked into Brad's eyes and said. "Okay."

Brad swallowed. He pulled his hands out of his pockets, finally, and circled Sebastian's waist. "Okay?"

Sebastian leaned into him. "I'll be with just you. Nobody else," he said against Brad's mouth. Then he nipped Brad's lower lip hard, making Brad jump. He was already strung taut, heart pounding in his ears, dick straining against his jeans, guts knotting up. The sting of Sebastian's teeth was somehow exactly what he needed, focusing him on the strangely pleasurable pain. Painful like the aching, addictive feeling of Sebastian pushing into him the first time. His breath sped up on a whine.

Sebastian smiled against his lips, then pulled back and looked at him, the smile melting away again. "If you hook up with anyone else, we're done."

Brad nodded, feeling like a bobble-head doll. "You trust me?"

Sebastian nodded back. He held Brad's face a little tighter. "You didn't have to tell me. It wouldn't have been wrong of you not to."

Brad wasn't sure why that would make Sebastian trust him. But he had a more pressing concern. "You forgive me?"

Sebastian looked at him in silence, while Brad's throat choked up on him. "Nothing to forgive, hon. You didn't do anything dishonest." Brad swallowed, saw Sebastian's eyes on his Adam's apple. "But you need that, yeah? I forgive you."

Brad felt weak with relief.

Sebastian leaned in and kissed him, a short kiss, tracing Brad's lips with his tongue. Brad gripped him tighter and tried to bring him into his body, but Sebastian pulled back one more time. "Now you're going to make it up to me."

Brad's heart jumped. "I am?"

Sebastian stepped back and smiled. Brad dropped his hands and waited.

"You're going to go into the bathroom, get your naked ass in the shower, and show me exactly what he did to you."

"Oh, fuck yes I am," he breathed, then hightailed it to the bathroom, losing his shirt somewhere on the way.

Chapter 22

Sebastian didn't let Brad come in the shower. He made him get out and lie on the bed, Sebastian toweling off slowly next to him, Brad watching, breath hitching and hips unable to stay still. Then Sebastian straddled Brad's legs and started tracing Brad's muscles with his tongue, licking the water off his skin.

"Oh, God," Brad whispered when Sebastian's tongue flicked across his nipple. Sebastian laughed softly against it, his lips vibrating, making Brad curl up in reaction, gasping.

Was this what it had felt like when Sebastian's cock had been in his mouth and he'd been moaning? Sebastian had liked that.

Brad had fucking loved it. Loved being on his knees in front of him. Loved the taste of Sebastian's pre-cum and the feel of him in his mouth. The gagging he could have done without, but Sebastian told him to use his hand to keep from taking him too deep and he'd gotten over it. Fast. Mostly after that, it had been about learning Sebastian with his tongue. The smooth head and the veiny shaft and that almost-not-there taste of copper when Brad pressed hard against the big blood vessel on the underside of Sebastian's cock. Sebastian's murmured instructions, and later his moans, made Brad moan in turn. Clutching Sebastian's shaft in one hand, his hip in the other. The taste of Sebastian when he came in Brad's mouth, Sebastian's hands somehow gripping his short hair tight.

Sebastian started licking down from Brad's navel. He wrapped his fingers around Brad's cock, holding him out of the way so he could tease around the base. Brad rocked his hips, trying to get Sebastian's fingers to tighten up or move or *something*. Sebastian nipped his hip bone hard and Brad stopped rocking, tried to be still, all his muscles locked up.

Finally, Sebastian looked up at him, Brad craning his neck to see, and he licked slowly along the slit in Brad's cockhead. Through the blood rushing in Brad's ears, he heard Sebastian ask, "Like this? Did he lick you like this?"

Brad nodded, doing his bobble-head imitation again. Sebastian started going through what Collin had done, step by step, like he was trying to write over Brad's memory of it. The same way he'd made Brad suck him in the shower before they got too into now to bother with what had happened then. Sebastian licked him and finally took him into his mouth. Brad's hips jerked, shoving his dick farther into Sebastian. He took Brad easily, but placed both hands on Brad's hips to keep him still, leaning in.

After that, it was sucking and swallowing and wet heat and then a finger up his ass, looking for his prostate. Pressing on it while Sebastian took Brad into his throat, and Brad lost it, coming so hard he couldn't hear himself shout. Everything went black and white and he curled up, his muscles beyond his control, feeling like he was emptying out. Way more than just cum. Trying to leave part of himself in Sebastian.

Sebastian gently pulled his finger out of Brad's ass, making his sphincter clench and a small aftershock quake in his balls. Sebastian pulled his mouth slowly off Brad, then licked him and kissed him until Brad's breathing evened out. Then Sebastian laid his head on Brad's thigh, stroking Brad's hip. Occasionally pressing kisses into his skin while Brad stroked Sebastian's hair.

Suddenly Brad had a lump in his throat. There was so much he wanted to say, and it was too soon and he didn't have the right and he probably wasn't good enough anyway. He swallowed around it and said, "I don't really deserve this."

Sebastian rose up on his elbows and looked up at Brad. "Deserve this what?"

"You."

"Why not?"

"I used a lot of girls in the past, trying to figure my shit out. My sisters say I was an asshole."

Sebastian pulled himself up next to Brad, propping his head on a hand to look down at him. He had that smile that knotted Brad up inside. "So, is it true?"

Brad shrugged, uncomfortable. Why did he feel like he had to be honest with Sebastian? But he was, like, unable to lie to Sebastian and didn't have a fucking clue why. Even if it was humiliating as shit.

"Maybe."

Sebastian just looked down at him in that calm way he had.

Brad sighed and gulped in a breath, holding it. "I just . . . I didn't really know what I wanted, you know? But I wasn't getting it, no matter who I slept with or whatever. I saw my sisters over spring break and they were giving me shit over it, saying I was using girls and . . ." he shrugged. "I don't know."

"Did you lie to anyone?"

Brad cringed. "I've tried not to the last couple years, but I wasn't so honest in high school. I might have let some girls think I was interested in, you know, more."

"But you weren't."

"It was so fucked up, you know? I'd think maybe this girl would do it for me, and then about two minutes after I came I'd be scrambling out of there, feeling like there was something wrong with me. All my friends thought getting some was, like, the pinnacle of existence and I was, like, 'meh.' So I faked it. Except I kept trying to find it, too."

Sebastian reached one finger out and traced Brad's jaw, following the finger with his eyes. "You maybe hurt some people, yeah?" he asked.

Brad thought of Ashley's face when he'd dumped her. Sebastian laid a very light finger on his Adam's apple as Brad swallowed. "Yeah." He paused. "I thought when I came over here you'd kick me out because of that thing with Collin. Like I didn't really deserve to be with you because I've been so, I don't know. Uncaring. Like I have bad karma."

"I'm glad you told me." Sebastian's voice was low. He was still watching his finger trace muscles in Brad's throat.

"Yeah?"

"Yeah." Sebastian looked at him again, into his eyes. "I didn't like that, thinking about you with some other guy, though." Nearly whispering, finger light on Brad's carotid artery.

"I can't stand thinking of you with someone else." Brad felt like he'd maybe ripped his chest open and invited Sebastian to poke around inside. He held his breath.

"I haven't been. Not since the first time with you."

Brad's breath left him in a whoosh. He would have collapsed onto the bed if he hadn't already been flat on his back in it.

"I can't absolve you of guilt for all those girls you might have hurt, hon, but I'm sure as hell not going to kick you out of bed for it, either. You have to work out how you want to deal with your past for yourself."

"I can do that." He hoped.

"I have to leave for class in an hour," Sebastian's voice brought Brad's attention back from wherever it had gone. They'd been talking, then he'd sort of dozed off. He rubbed his eyes and looked at Sebastian's clock, trying not to dislodge Sebastian's arm from his waist. He liked Sebastian spooning him.

"Yeah, I have a class this afternoon I can't miss. I'll need to leave about then, too."

"What kinda class? Some phys ed health thing?" Sebastian sounded honestly curious.

Which made it a little easier to say, "Organic gardening." He held his breath, waiting for a response.

"Really? That sounds cool. I didn't know Calapooya even had an ag program."

Brad scrunched his eyes closed. "It's a home ec class."

Sebastian loomed over him suddenly, looking down at him. "Brad, are you a home ec major?" he asked, playfully mocking. Brad knew that when he looked up he'd see Sebastian's mischievous smile that made him gooey inside.

Yep, there it was. "Family and consumer sciences. It's my minor," he admitted.

Sebastian's eyes lit up even more. "Sounds like home ec. Bet that makes you popular at the frat house."

Brad couldn't help but smile back. "It does. I'm in charge of the kitchen."

"What, like you cook and stuff?"

"Not usually. We have a cook, but I plan the menus and make sure he has all the stuff he needs. Sometimes I cook for formal dinners."

Was that weird? Some of the frat guys thought it was, but no one ever said shit to his face once they tasted what he produced.

Sebastian cocked his head, looking less playful and more interested. "You really love it, yeah? Cooking."

No one, *no one*, had ever just recognized that. Even his mom and his sisters thought it was some kind of charming, eccentric hobby for him. Brad swallowed. "Yeah," he said, his voice gravelly from being forced out past some sort of blockage.

"Better than all your jock stuff?" Sebastian looked much more serious now.

"Yeah." Brad swallowed again.

"How come you aren't majoring in it? Or in a cooking school?"

Brad swallowed a third time and had to look away. Before he had to work up some kind of answer, Sebastian said softly, lowering his head, "Yeah, that might be hard for people to understand about you. My poor, misunderstood jock." Murmuring in Brad's ear. Then kissing along his cheekbone. His eyelid. "Let me take your mind off that, honey." He returned to Brad's earlobe, tonguing it.

"Please," Brad groaned.

"On your stomach, then."

Sebastian pushed lightly on his shoulder. Brad rolled over immediately and stretched against the sheets. Sebastian had barely even touched him, but the blood was already pumping into his cock. He squirmed. Sebastian laid a palm on the small of Brad's back. "Keep still, Bradley."

"Mmm. Like it when you call me that."

"Yeah?" Sebastian murmured in his ear, chest pressed against Brad's back. "Good, because I'm not stopping anytime soon."

"You know it's not really my name."

"That's okay," Sebastian said into Brad's spine in between kisses. "It's my name for you. Today, Bradley"—he kissed Brad's lower back, making Brad clench his muscles —"I'm going to teach you all about rimming."

Brad learned rimming was hot breath on his sacrum, Sebastian's thumbs pulling his cheeks open, exposing his asshole. Brushing a finger around it, making Brad clench and push his hips up, trying to get more. Sebastian ringing it with small licks and quick flicks of his tongue, more tease than touch. Finally Sebastian's tongue licking and twisting inside him, then stroking into him. Then a finger, Sebastian's tongue easing the way.

Brad couldn't stop moving, clutching the sheets and sweating into them by the time Sebastian pulled himself up to whisper "I want to fuck you," in Brad's ear, carefully stretching him with more fingers. Brad moaned and nodded. Within seconds, Sebastian had lubed him up and put on a condom, then pushed slowly into Brad.

It was better than the first time. The head of Sebastian's dick stroked his prostate with what felt like every thrust, and each time it rubbed across his gland, the sharp edge of orgasm tugged at him. Like he was at the top of a carnival ride, waiting for it to start. He hung on until Sebastian pushed up on shaking arms over Brad and moved in short hard thrusts. "Stroke yourself, Bradley," he gasped. "Come for me."

Brad let go of the pillow he was mangling and snaked a hand around himself, pulling hard just a couple of times before yelling and writhing, clamping down on Sebastian's dick in his ass and pumping a bucket-load of pleasure into the bedding. Sebastian came just after, pulsing inside him and heat rushing into him, trapped by the condom.

Sebastian collapsed on top of him and they breathed with each other for a while.

If he'd done all this when he should have, back in high school, would it have been this good? Based on what had happened with Collin, Brad was thinking no. The amazing intensity was because he was doing it with Sebastian.

"You have the most beautiful ass, hon," Sebastian mumbled into the back of Brad's neck.

Brad smiled what was probably a goofy-looking smile. "Yeah?"

"Mmm." Sebastian nodded against him. "Tight and round. Perfect bubble butt."

"That's good?"

"So good," Sebastian groaned. "Like someone took a blueprint of my fantasy ass and made yours just for me."

Brad squeezed all his butt muscles tight, clenching around Sebastian.

"Mmm. There's something we'll explore in the future." He was downright purring into Brad's skin, now.

"What?"

"You're going to learn how to have a beautiful, *active* ass, Bradley."

Chapter 23

Collin was waiting for Brad when he got back to the frat house after Organic Gardening. He looked like he was just hanging on the porch, doing some homework, but since it was about fifty-five degrees out, Brad figured that was just an act. Although the sun was occasionally peeking through the clouds.

As he walked up the steps, Collin closed his textbook and put away his notes. Brad stopped at the top step and looked at him. "Hey."

Collin stood up. "Hey."

"Guess we should go get a beer or something, huh?" Brad wanted to get this out of the way. Hopefully, he wouldn't have to move into a new room or something. Although if he could get a room of his own on the top floor, and he managed to sneak Sebastian in . . . Nah. That was stupid.

"I think that might be a good idea." Collin just left his stuff on the porch and they took off. They didn't go to the keg fridge in the frat's basement or the bar around the corner; they headed for the one around the corner from that. They might still run into guys they knew, maybe from other frats, but it was only four o'clock. They'd be able to find someplace to talk, some dark corner. It was a dive bar, perfect for secrets.

Collin walked fast, hands stuffed in his pockets, nervous energy all hanging out. Brad decided it was Collin's show. He'd just wait and see.

After they passed the first bar, Collin finally spoke up. "I'm sorry." He was walking along next to Brad, doing some weird fidgety thing: tucking his chin into his zipped-up coat collar, then pulling it out, over and over. Brad had never noticed Collin was so much shorter than him. Couldn't be more than five eight. Couple inches shorter than Sebastian.

"You said that already. Don't be sorry. You're good at it." *Not as good as Sebastian.*

Collin's chin popped out of his collar and he stopped walking to turn to Brad. He looked kind of like a startled turtle. "Uh, thanks." He sighed and ran a hand through his hair, looking off to the side for a second. "Listen, it's not exactly like I made it sound, man. I mean, I sounded all into you, and I was, I guess, but I've had all day to think about it . . ."

Brad nudged Collin's arm with his elbow, and they slowly started toward the bar again. Brad tried to figure out exactly what he needed to ask. "Okay, so what'd you work out?"

"I figured out I'm secretary of this fucking frat but I feel like I'm pretending to be something I'm not."

It took Brad a minute. *Oh, duh.* "'Cause you're gay and no one knows."

"Yeah. Just, I ended up here and I knew I was gay, but I wanted to be part of a group of brothers or something. I thought I'd just feel it out, maybe figure out a way to tell everyone. But as soon as I became active, I was voted Pledge Chair, and since then it's seemed like it's not such a great idea to tell everyone I don't want to hear them calling anyone a fucking faggot anymore." Collin's voice, sad at the start, had turned bitter and caustic.

"Dude, you knew you were gay and you chose this frat? I wouldn't have done that."

"You didn't think you were gay when you rushed?"

"Not really. I mean, I felt different, I guess. I don't know." Brad shrugged and kicked at a rock in the sidewalk.

Collin nodded. "I getcha."

He probably did.

They reached the door of the falling-down, dismal, gray-peeling-paint dive they'd been heading toward. Brad stopped and looked around. It was kind of a nice day, really. You didn't get a lot of nice days around here in the spring. One of those days where the clouds looked like rain, but you knew they wouldn't dare, with the sun always peeking through and making everything buttery yellow. "You really wanna go in there?"

"Nah. We'll get plenty to drink later. Tonight's our second rush party."

"Shit," Brad groaned. He was always forgetting about frat obligations unless it was something he had to help with. He made it a point to help as little as possible. He never remembered rush parties because food was almost an afterthought, so he didn't have to be involved in the planning. As long as there was enough beer, things were good.

They turned around and walked slowly back. Brad watched his feet scuff the ground while Collin went on. "My uncle was in Theta Alpha Gamma, and he wanted me to be in it, too. We've always been close and he doesn't have any kids, so I figured if I was going to join one anyway, make him happy. But fuck, man, I've been living in the house for a year, been active for almost two, I've held, like, ten different offices, and I feel completely isolated. You know?"

Well, Brad could lie, but, "Not really." Collin scowled at him, so he tried to explain. "Dude, I joined because I needed cheap housing and they offered me a scholarship if I'd pledge. I never really cared about brotherhood stuff before I pledged, and after, it was sort of a bonus. I guess maybe I felt it at first, but not so much lately." Weird, he hadn't even noticed that.

"That's the first thing that made me think you might be gay."

"What?"

"You started isolating yourself. My first year you were more involved and you hung out a lot, but now if it's not in the kitchen or part of the morning workouts, you avoid it. You even started being kind of a dick to Kyle."

"Yeah," Brad said softly, "guess I have."

"One day about a month ago, Eddie was giving you shit in the TV room about some girl he hooked up with and you said, 'You can have her, man.'"

"*That's* what made you sure I was gay? Pretty thin."

"You looked at my ass every single time I bent over in the shower, dude."

"I *knew* you were doing that on purpose! Fuck! Of course I looked."

Collin was smiling, but trying to hide it in his collar. Sort of trying to hide it. He slowed down, the smile melting off. He started kicking the ground. "Nah. It was when I placed that stupid bet, you know? I didn't even mean to; Ricky was going on about it. Asking me what I thought. It just sort of slipped out."

"Then a twenty slipped out of your wallet?"

Collin flushed and glanced at Brad. "Yeah. After that, you started being weird around me. Sorry."

"S'okay, man." Surprisingly, he actually meant it.

Even though they'd been walking slowly, they were less than a block from the house now. "Listen, I thought: you were gay, I was gay, we're in the same frat; let's be gay together," Collin said quickly. Brad looked at him skeptically. "And yeah, I like you," Collin admitted. "But I'm not, like, broken-hearted. I'm lonely."

So he was looking for love in other places? "You hooking up with Toby?"

"Just that one night: the party. You went after Sebastian that night, didn't you?"

"Yeah." They stopped next to a telephone pole for a minute, within sight of the house. He didn't think Collin had said everything he wanted to say, and Brad had something he wanted to know. He started to ask, but Collin beat him to it.

"You work things out with him?"

Oh, man. There was Brad's goofy smile again. He looked at the ground, embarrassed. Collin snorted softly and looked away. "Yeah," Brad told him finally.

"Good. Really, I mean it. You seem kinda into him," he added dryly.

Brad bit his lips together to keep from smiling more. He needed a change of subject, and maybe someone else's opinion. "You ever think about coming out to the frat now?"

Collin looked startled. "Not anymore. Maybe if I wasn't so involved."

Brad nodded and looked up at the frat house. It was nearly the same color as that dive bar. Another thing he'd never noticed before. At least it was in better shape. Kind of.

"Are you thinking about it?" Collin asked.

"I don't know."

"Fuck," Collin muttered to the telephone pole. "Every time I think about how the guys might react . . . I think I'm giving myself an ulcer."

"Yeah, see, that's the thing. I guess I'm not really sure I care how they react."

"Hey!" They both turned to the frat at Julian's yell. He was standing on the porch in yellow rubber gloves and an apron. "Get your asses in here and help us get ready for this party tonight!" Then he turned and stomped back inside.

"You ever think Jules's gay?" Brad asked as they started toward the house again.

Collin snorted. "No."

Chapter 24

Sebastian spent a lazy Sunday morning watching Brad work in his kitchen, making blueberry pancakes with maple syrup and bacon for breakfast. The pancakes were nearly freaking orgasmic. They would have been *truly* orgasmic if he'd eaten them off Brad's naked body.

Unfortunately, his roommates were there.

Brad made enough blueberry pancakes for them, too. He set a stacked serving plate on the table, then sat down to eat with Sebastian and Toby. Paul wandered in, scowled in Brad's general direction, and said, "Morning, Sebastian. Hey, Toby."

Sebastian looked up at Paul pointedly, looked at Brad, then looked back at Paul. Paul ignored him and sat down at the table, muttering to himself.

Toby kept his head down, shoveling in pancakes. Like he wanted to get while the getting was good and then get gone.

Sebastian watched Brad. Instead of seeming pissed or any of the other things Sebastian found himself worried about—confused or stunned or, worst of all, hurt—Brad looked amused. He stayed amused all through the mutterings and scowling. Then Paul said, "Where'd these pancakes come from?"

Sebastian found it hard to be as amused by Paul's sucky attitude as Brad was. He smiled now, though. Broadly. "Brad made them. He's a really good cook, yeah?"

"They're awful," Paul said nastily, then took another two from the serving plate and picked up the syrup pitcher.

Just as the syrup started oozing out, Brad grabbed the plate out from under the pitcher and took it to the garbage.

Paul stared, surprised, as the syrup poured out on the table. "Hey!" He hastily set the pitcher down and stood up, shoving his chair back and turning to Brad. Toby finally stopped pretending to be deaf and dumb and looked up in interest.

Brad very deliberately stared at Paul as he dumped the pancakes in the garbage. The expression on his face was pretty scary, and Paul wisely stayed quiet. He still looked pissed, though, hands fisted, teeth clenched.

It appeared Brad didn't take insults to his cooking skills well.

Once the pancakes had splatted their way into the garbage, Brad took the plate to the sink, rinsed it, and then got a washcloth wet. He carried it, dripping, to Paul and dropped it on the table in front of him. "When you're done cleaning up your mess, you're excused."

Paul turned red. He sputtered at Brad a few seconds before he rounded on Sebastian. "If you're going to have jocks over, you could at least make them behave!"

Then he stomped out of the room.

Toby snorted. "Paul's whack."

Brad sat back down, but he wasn't eating, he was just looking at his plate.

"Sorry about that," Sebastian said.

Brad finally looked at him. He appeared annoyed and disgusted, but not hurt. Sebastian's breath came a little easier. He wasn't sure how to fix a hurt Brad. Well, except for taking him back to bed. "I'm not cleaning it up," he told Sebastian.

Sebastian shrugged. "I say we leave it for Paul."

"Fine with me," Toby said between bites. He swallowed his last mouthful of food and wiped his face, then leaned back in his chair and smiled as only the well-fed grad student could. "Frat Boy, those were some amazing pancakes. Feel free to stay overnight anytime."

Sebastian lifted an eyebrow at Brad as Toby wandered out of the room. Brad shrugged. "It's a better nickname than my fraternity brothers gave me."

"Which was?"

"At first they called me 'Fellator.' 'Cause of my last name, you know? Feller; Fellator."

Sebastian grinned at him. "Yeah, but what do they call you now?"

Brad turned pink and cleared his throat. "Um, they call me Alpha Dawg."

Sebastian stood up and rounded the table, draped his arms over Brad's shoulders and leaned down to speak in his ear. Brad tilted his head to make room for him. "Oh, but honey, they have that wrong.

You're not the alpha dog. I am." He caught Brad's earlobe between his teeth and watched goosebumps prickle Brad's skin.

"Yeah," Brad agreed. "I think you are."

Sebastian took Brad back to bed.

ΘΑΓ

Brad didn't go back to the frat until Sunday evening. He'd finished his homework at Sebastian's. Then Sebastian had rewarded him for being a good student.

He'd been wearing his glasses while rewarding Brad.

Brad wanted to be a good student again at the earliest opportunity.

Back at TAG house, as Brad was walking up the stairs, Ashley was skipping down them, smiling and humming to herself. She looked up and saw Brad, smiling bigger.

Then she recognized him. "Shit," she muttered.

Brad cleared his throat and rubbed his ear. "Uh, hey, Ashley."

"Brad." She nodded. Then flicked a look over his shoulder. The smile came back, but it was fake now. Julian was probably down there.

"Hanging out with Kyle?"

"Yeah." Some of her real smile fought its way back. "Collin was gone all afternoon, too. We just hung out and, um, studied."

Julian had a coughing fit behind them. Ashley snorted at him.

"Brad, you know how we were talking about getting together for coffee sometime and talking?"

"Uh—"

"Now's a great time for me. How about you?"

"Well, I was—"

"Great! Meet me in the coffee shop where we met last week. I'll take the same thing. Half-hour? Good." As she spoke, she bounced down the stairs. Then she breezed past Julian, nose in the air, and slammed out the door.

Brad was confused as hell, but he had a feeling it would be easier for him in the long run if he showed up at the café and played nice. What the hell, it would make Kyle happy. This time, he was very, very careful to make sure he didn't put too much cream in her coffee. But when she arrived and peeled off the lid, she wrinkled her nose at him. "I knew last time was an accident."

"Wha . . .?"

Ashley didn't explain. She just got up and put more cream in.

When she sat back down, she blew on her coffee, took a sip, set it down, carefully folded her hands on the table, and looked at Brad. "Well."

"Yeeeeah." Brad nodded at her. *Well what?*

"So. I guess Kyle talked to you."

"We talk all the time. He's my roommate." This was getting bizarre.

She scowled at him. "About *me*, Brad."

"Oh! Oh, yeah. I told him I was fine with it if you guys are seeing each other."

"Good." Some of that smile was fighting its way out again. "I really like him. It would suck if you were going to make trouble for me."

"Why would I make trouble for you? I was the asshole there."

She nodded thoughtfully. "True. But you never know what goes through a guy's mind." She sighed soulfully, making little designs on the tabletop with her index finger.

Brad nodded again. He didn't know why. "You like Kyle?"

The smile bloomed on her face. He had the feeling he was looking at the same smile he got on his face when he thought about Sebastian. "Uh-huh." She nodded, looking down. "You like Sebastian?"

Shit. Blushing *and* smiling. Brad looked down. He was acting like a girl.

He probably didn't need to share that sentiment.

Ashley sighed, a touch exasperated. "You know that friends thing?"

"Uh, yeah." *What friends thing?*

"I guess we could try it. Being friends."

Brad looked up, a little shocked. Not so much at the offer, but at his reaction: he wasn't alarmed by the idea. "Yeah. Okay. We could try it."

Chapter 25

On Monday morning, Brad went running with the guys. Somewhere along the way, he got separated from the frat pack and then got "lost." Fortunately, he found his way to Sebastian's.

"Mmm, sweaty man," Sebastian said when he opened the door and pulled Brad into his room.

The same thing happened Wednesday.

No one was really checking up on his whereabouts, but Kyle had noticed something was off by Friday morning.

"Dude, let me see if I understand this," Kyle said, eying Brad from his bed. "Even though we're about to go for our morning run, you just took a shower."

"Yep. And you're still not up." Brad dug around in his closet for his running shoes. He'd just worn them Wednesday; where were they?

Kyle ignored Brad's second comment. "Okay, and can I assume by the time the other guys and me wind up our run at the gym to shower, you will have mysteriously disappeared? Again? Just like on Monday and Wednesday?"

"You may assume so." Brad found his shoes and sat on the floor to lace them up. "You better get moving, I'm almost ready." Kyle was sitting up now, but covered by the blanket from the waist down, his light brown hair sticking up everywhere. He was looking at Brad like he'd grown another head.

"What is up with you? Are you involved in something illegal?"

Brad scoffed. "No!" Homosexual acts weren't illegal anymore, right? Brad straightened up, done tying his shoes. "The fuck, man?"

"Dude, I don't know how to explain it! If it was a chick, you'd bring her around. If you had a secret love child . . . I don't know what you'd do, but I don't think it would involve Monday, Wednesday, and Friday mornings. Hey!" He pointed an accusing finger at Brad. "And you were gone all last Saturday night, too. It's not a job, 'cause you're still always broke. It's not syphilis, 'cause you aren't foaming at the mouth. The fuck are you up to, Brad?"

"I'm seeing someone."

"What, you mean like dating?"

"Yeah."

"So bring her around and end the mystery. Whoever bet you have a secret girlfriend wins the pool and you can stop hiding. Oh, but you know, we should figure out who that is and get you a cut of the winnings before you show up with her. It could be a lot of—"

"No."

"You don't want any of the money?"

"I'm not bringing the person I'm seeing over to meet everyone or hang out or whatever."

Kyle stared at him, wrinkling his brow. "Dude, we don't care if she's kinda ugly. Not every girl can be as hot as Ashley. If you like her . . ."

Brad laughed shortly and stood up. "Ugly's got nothing to do with it. I'm going to go stretch; Collin's all ready to go. You have five minutes or we leave you behind." He walked out the door and shut it on whatever Kyle was starting to say next.

When he got to Sebastian's, Sebastian answered the door with bedhead and whiskers. He didn't say anything, just pulled Brad through the door and started kissing him, then walked him backward to the bed.

Later, when Brad was naked on his knees before Sebastian, running his tongue around Sebastian's flared head, he glanced up and saw Sebastian watching him. Brown eyes focused on Brad's as he gripped the back of Brad's head and guided his cock into Brad's mouth.

Brad couldn't look away. Sebastian seemed so *right* up there, watching him. Directing Brad's head, occasionally murmuring to him, telling him how good he was. Praising him.

I'd do anything he wants.

And he did. When Sebastian slowly pushed farther into Brad's mouth and said, "Bradley, you're going to take me into your throat, yeah? You want to, honey; I can see it," Brad moaned. Oh fuck yeah, he wanted. His fingers dug into the backs of Sebastian's thighs as he looked into Sebastian's eyes and waited.

Sebastian placed his hands on either side of Brad's head, gripping him tightly. "You want this?"

Brad managed a quick nod.

"Brad, if you need me to stop, just push me off you, yeah? Don't let me hurt you. Right before you feel me shove into your throat, you need to take a breath, hon. I'll tell you when. You won't be able to breathe when you have my dick that deep in you."

Brad shuddered, and his asshole clenched up in sympathy with his throat. Or maybe it was jealous. He made one of those noises he couldn't control, trying to tell Sebastian with his eyes how much he wanted it.

Sebastian ran his thumbs down Brad's cheekbones, stroking him. "Good boy."

Brad shuddered again. Remembered the day he'd fantasized about Sebastian punishing him. Sebastian started to rock his hips in and out, letting Brad get used to the feeling of his head all the way in the back of his mouth. Brad flattened his tongue out along the underside; no room for it with Sebastian's cock there. Within a few minutes, he was breathing heavy.

"Take a breath, Bradley," Sebastian whispered, gasping.

Brad sucked in a lungful of air, and Sebastian rammed his cock into Brad's throat. Brad tried to yell, but he couldn't. The trapped yell was part instinct and part gut-clenching want. Sebastian kept watching his eyes, his mouth hanging open while he panted, fucking in and out of Brad's throat.

Maybe he should have resented it or fought it, but he wanted it. He managed a few breaths, but mostly it was just taking Sebastian into him how Sebastian wanted. When Sebastian choked out, "Now, hon," and Brad felt Sebastian's cum warm his throat, Sebastian's hands holding him tight, his nuts pulled up and he came, too. Sebastian eased back enough so Brad could breathe, and Brad moaned out the rest of his orgasm.

Sebastian sat down hard on the floor next to him, pulling Brad close. Wrapping his arms around Brad and holding him tight, resting Brad's head on his shoulder. Calling him honey and kissing his hair.

When their breaths had mostly slowed down and Sebastian had scooted them back so he could lean on the bed, he asked, "Was that too rough?"

Brad shook his head and continued swirling a finger in Sebastian's chest hair. He cleared his throat. Then he had to again before he could rasp, "I liked it."

"You wanna get in the bed, hon?"

Brad pressed his forehead against Sebastian's neck and traced Sebastian's abdominal muscles with his fingertips. "I wanna talk to you about something." He sounded like he smoked a pack a day.

"'Kay." Sebastian kissed his head again.

"You remember when I plagiarized that paper?"

Sebastian's voice deepened as he said, "I'm not likely to forget it, hon."

Brad cringed, but pulled his head off Sebastian's chest and looked at him. He looked very serious.

"I still feel guilty about that. I've never done it before, not even in other classes—"

"I know."

"I think I still need to deal with it—the guilt."

Sebastian's eyes searched his. "Yeah?"

"What if I did some sort of penance?"

Sebastian blinked and let out a breath. "Like what?"

"What'd you think I was going to say?" Brad stretched and lay on the floor on his back, arms pillowing his head.

Sebastian lay on his side next to him, propping his head on his hand. "I don't know." He started running his fingers along Brad's ribs. "I was just worried you felt like you needed to move on. I'm not really ready for that yet."

Brad stared at him a long moment. "You aren't?" He pushed himself up, tensing his abs and stretching to reach Sebastian's mouth. Palmed Sebastian's cheek and kissed him slowly.

"No."

"How would moving on help me do penance?"

Sebastian's smile appeared, the one Brad liked so much. This time it seemed like he was mocking himself. "People talk themselves into weird shit. You managed to convince yourself you weren't attracted to guys until you were twenty-one."

Brad just snorted. His abs got tired, so he lay back down.

"Okay, so tell me about doing penance. For forgiveness, yeah?" Sebastian asked.

"Forgiveness." Brad nodded solemnly. Sebastian smiled that smile, looking down at him. "You're my confessor. You know about my sin and now you can assign me some penitential act."

Sebastian nodded, his smile growing into a grin. "If necessary, I could help you carry out your penance." With his scruffy whiskers and his hair sticking up, he looked demonic. Like a queer incubus.

Brad nodded again. "Kinda like a priest."

Sebastian's smile loomed larger as he leaned down. Nearly to Brad's lips he said, "A wicked, perverted, yet sexy priest. A priest with toys."

Brad shivered. "I'm really feeling the need for forgiveness," he whispered before Sebastian kissed him.

Chapter 26

Friday afternoon, after Organic Gardening, Brad went back to the frat, took a shower, stuffed some extra clothes, his razor, his toothbrush, and his history texts in his backpack, and left for Sebastian's. Just like Sebastian had told him to. "So you can start repenting," he'd said. "It's a good night for it; Toby and Paul are going out."

Brad really, really wanted to repent. He *needed* it.

He was *vibrating* with the need to repent.

When he knocked on the door, Sebastian opened it with a very satyr-esque smile. It was a new smile: Sebastian's "wicked priest" smile. Brad's blood started pounding. He liked that smile more than the teasing smile. He *needed* that smile.

Sebastian held out his hand, not saying anything, and pulled Brad into the bedroom. "Strip and get on the bed, Bradley. Hands and knees."

Brad had a hard time taking in enough oxygen. He dropped his backpack on the floor and pulled his shirt over his head. Sebastian stood in front of him, watching him with that smile, and by the time Brad squatted to untie his shoes, he was fully hard.

"No, Bradley." Fuck. That voice. "Jeans first."

"But—"

"No."

Brad swallowed and stood back up. His fingers had a hard time with his fly, but he eventually got it, looking into Sebastian's eyes as he eased the denim past his hips.

"Stop," Sebastian ordered when Brad had his pants hanging at mid-thigh. "Mmm, you look hot in those, hon. Did you get them just for me?"

"Yeah," Brad croaked. He'd watched himself pull the boxer briefs on a half hour before, looking at the way they stretched over his ass and hugged his package. Just the thought of wearing them for Sebastian had made him half-hard.

Sebastian amped up the smile, one corner of his mouth curling up a little more. His eyes tracked all over Brad's body as he slowly walked around to stand behind Brad. He trailed a hand across Brad's ass, making Brad clench his muscles all up his back.

"Pull down your boxers, Bradley," Sebastian said quietly. Brad felt him watching as he bent to pull them down to his knees with his jeans.

"Now your shoes." Brad started to squat. "No, bend over."

When Brad took a shuddery breath and bent over in front of Sebastian, Sebastian's hands stroked over his lower back.

"Did you get all clean for me?"

"Yeah," Brad choked. His fingers stopped taking messages from his central nervous system.

"Mmm. Let's see about that," Sebastian drawled, voice as slow as his hands trailing down to grip Brad's cheeks. "Keep working on those shoes, hon," he whispered.

Brad closed his eyes and nearly toppled over. He planted one hand on the floor to keep himself up. How was he supposed to get his shoes off with Sebastian standing behind him, doing incredibly nasty things? Digging his thumbs into Brad's crack, pulling him wide open, brushing a thumb across his asshole. Inspecting him.

Then Sebastian let go of him. He slapped a cheek once, hard, surprising a squeak out of Brad.

"C'mon. Naked on the bed. Now."

Brad didn't remember how, but he got his shoes and clothes off, even knowing Sebastian was standing behind him, watching his muscles work and his balls swing and jiggle between his legs. He could feel Sebastian's eyes all over him as he crawled onto the bed, quivering by the time he was on all fours, staring at the wall, waiting.

"Fuck, that's so hot." Sebastian sounded a little choked. Brad closed his eyes and dropped his head between his arms. Behind him, he heard Sebastian getting something out of the nightstand, then dropping it on the bed. He opened his eyes and looked between his legs. Lube. And that was . . . oh fuck. A butt plug. Brad's elbows gave out, his face and shoulders hitting the bed.

"Bradley," Sebastian said softly. "I want you to hold yourself open for me. Can you do that, hon?"

Brad sucked in an involuntary breath, face mashing against the sheet. He brought his shaking hands back and grabbed his cheeks, spreading himself wide for Sebastian. He managed not to beg Sebastian to touch him, but it was a near thing. He ground his forehead into the bed, gritting his teeth.

Sebastian's clothes rustled as he bent forward, and hot breath fell on the end of Brad's spine. Just like the first time Sebastian had kissed him there. "Please," Brad gasped when Sebastian's lips touched his hole. He felt Sebastian's mouth stretch into a smile, the scrape of stubble on the sensitive skin behind his balls. Brad shuddered out a groan.

Oh God, Sebastian's tongue was hot and wet and slippery, sliding around all the little puckers and folds. Brad nearly sobbed, his breath hitching uncontrollably in his chest as Sebastian's tongue licked inside him, the gentle raspy slide in and out making him rock back. He could come from just this, he knew he could. He'd do anything if it just. Wouldn't. Stop.

Sebastian stopped.

"Uuuuh," Brad whined. The most coherent protest he could make.

Sebastian laughed softly. "S'okay, honey, there's more. But you don't get to come for a long, long time. Penance, remember?"

Brad groaned. He dug his fingers into his ass cheeks harder.

"Stay just like this, Bradley," Sebastian whispered, sliding up on the bed next to Brad, on his side. He palmed the back of Brad's head and turned it toward him, kissing him. Brad tasted himself on Sebastian's tongue as Sebastian fed it to him. He sucked on it until Sebastian made him stop.

Then Sebastian slid off the bed, standing behind Brad again. Brad closed his eyes and trembled. He heard Sebastian open the lube, and his asshole clenched, desperately trying to get Sebastian's attention. "Mmm, tempting, hon. But you're doing penance."

Brad whined at him again. Sebastian chuckled, and then suddenly something was pushing into Brad's ass. He had a vivid flash of fucking himself with the hairbrush, wishing it was Seb, and he nearly cried out.

The plug was bigger than the hairbrush, and Sebastian hadn't stretched him, really. "Tell me it if hurts too much, honey. It should hurt some though, or you aren't doing proper penance."

"Nnnngh. So good," Brad panted. It burned in a way he hadn't felt since those first couple of times, stretching him wider as Sebastian slowly pushed it in. Then the plug was inside him, narrowing before the base lodged in his crack. Sebastian tapped on it, and Brad felt it against his sweet spot. "Oh, fuck, Sebastian. So good." No idea if he was even intelligible.

He was shaking, so turned on his heart beat out his ears and in his feet and most of all in his cock. Sebastian rubbed the small of his back soothingly, prickling his skin with goosebumps. He started to come down, his heartbeat settling, his sweat soaking the sheets under his forehead and shoulders.

Sebastian's fingers interlaced with his, which were cramping, he'd been gripping his ass so hard. Sebastian carefully pulled them off, letting Brad's hands fall to the bed. He leaned in and kissed Brad where his fingers had been, making Brad whimper. "I think you gave yourself bruises, hon."

Sebastian rubbed farther up Brad's back, soothing him and gently pushing him over on his side. He lay down next to Brad again, looking into his eyes. "Feels all right?" he asked gently.

"Define all right," Brad croaked.

"Feels like maybe if you don't come soon you might die, but you aren't in pain?"

"Yeah," Brad breathed. "'S'all right."

Sebastian moved forward to kiss him. Brad wanted to grab him and pull him closer, but his muscles weren't back online yet. He whined again when Sebastian pulled back.

He was very whiny tonight.

Sebastian smiled and drew in a shuddery breath, sweat beading his forehead. He wasn't as in control as Brad had thought. Brad swallowed, wishing Sebastian would lose it completely but knowing it wasn't going to happen.

"On your back, hon. I don't need to tell you you can't touch yourself, yeah?" Brad shook his head, looking at Sebastian as he rolled onto his back, the plug inside him keeping him on edge. "That was so fucking hot." He straddled Brad's shoulders as he spoke. "Thought I might come in my jeans just watching that plug slide into your ass."

Brad opened his mouth, his breath coming faster again as Sebastian unzipped his jeans, his hard cock springing out. *Fuck, no underwear.* Brad closed his eyes.

"Eyes open, Bradley. Look at me." Brad's eyes popped open. Sebastian looked directly down at him. "I want you watching me when I come in your mouth." He gripped his shaft in one hand and traced Brad's lips with his head, smearing them with pre-cum. Brad moaned when Sebastian held still so he could lick it off of him. He slipped his tongue under the ridge and slid it into that little V on the underside. Sebastian's breath came in gasps now, his mouth open, eyelids heavy. Brad sealed his lips around Sebastian's head and sucked.

Sebastian groaned. "Wanna fuck your mouth. Shove myself into your throat."

Brad made a pleading sound, begging with his eyes.

"Can't, hon. You'll come. You don't get to come until after dinner." Brad felt his eyes go wide. He made a sound of protest. "Penance," Sebastian reminded him.

Brad groaned. Sebastian looked down at him, smiling the wicked priest smile. "I get to come now, though."

That was just cruel. And so hot Brad clenched his muscles around the plug inside him, making himself moan. Sebastian smiled wider, then canted himself forward, sliding farther into Brad's mouth as he reached to hold Brad's head still between his hands.

As Sebastian fucked his mouth, Brad couldn't stop his hips from thrusting. It was an automatic reaction, like a dog getting his sweet spot scratched. Sebastian's dick rubbed against the roof of Brad's mouth, pushing back almost until Brad gagged, then pulling out again. Brad slid his tongue along the underside, tasting that almost-copper flavor and sucking so hard his cheeks hollowed.

Within two minutes, Sebastian came in Brad's mouth, the warm rush hitting his tongue and his taste buds. Sebastian tasted a little bit bleachy and a little bit sweet. Brad was addicted to that flavor.

Sebastian hung over him, groaning as Brad tried to suck him dry. Brad looked into his eyes and held him in his mouth and thought he might just spontaneously combust. His ass was tingling and his back was arched and Sebastian's cock felt like the reason Brad had a mouth. He nearly cried when Sebastian panted his name, then brought a trembling hand to his cheek and stroked his face.

"Good boy. So fucking good." Sebastian eased himself out of Brad's mouth and collapsed on the bed next to him.

Brad whined again, and Sebastian stroked his chest clumsily. "'S'okay, hon. It won't be too long. I'll make it worth it."

Cooking dinner was bad. Sebastian made him get dressed before he went out to get started, and he kept coming up behind Brad and saying, "Let me make sure that plug's still there. Sometimes they slip out." Then torturing him by worming a hand down the back of his jeans to "check." Pushing in to make sure it hadn't slipped. Pulling on it to make sure it was "well-seated."

Thank God Brad had planned something simple for dinner. He even had the sauce pre-made.

Eating was worse. Brad sat in his chair and squirmed while Sebastian smiled the wicked priest smile. Every time Sebastian slipped his fork between his lips, Brad wanted to whimper. His ass throbbed around the plug. In time with his heart. Winding him up.

Penance was excruciatingly, tortuously exciting. He spent the hour they took for dinner on edge, breathing never quite normal, moving carefully. Caught between just wanting it to be over and wanting to make Sebastian happy. A number of times Brad thought he was about to come in his *penne all'arrabbiata*. He certainly wasn't eating it.

He managed to make it to the bedroom though, where Sebastian told him to strip and get on the bed, head on the sheets, ass in the air.

Sebastian didn't take anything off, just stood and watched Brad get naked. The slide of clothing against Brad's skin was enough to make him gasp, his cock so hard it jumped in time with his heartbeat. He climbed on the bed and assumed the position, pretty much exactly where he'd been an hour before. The sheet was even still damp under his cheek. Or maybe he'd started sweating all over again. He shivered.

Silently, Sebastian got undressed beside the bed, where Brad could see. Brad watched Sebastian put on a condom, then stroke his shaft with lube, wishing he was the one touching Sebastian like that.

Oh, yeah. Penance.

By the time Sebastian finally climbed on the bed, kneeling behind Brad, Brad was shaking again. He moaned when Sebastian eased out the plug. He moaned louder when Sebastian guided himself to his hole and started pushing in. It ached a little, the stretch, which just made the feeling of Sebastian entering him that much better.

Once Sebastian was fully inside, balls pressing against Brad, he leaned over him to say in Brad's ear, "Bradley, you can't touch yourself, and I won't be stroking you, either. You think you'll come for me, honey?"

"Yes." He barely got it out.

"Good boy."

Instead of pounding into him like Brad thought he wanted, Sebastian moved slowly and gently, every stroke long, Sebastian almost pulling out, then pushing all the way back in. Brad twisted his hands into the sheets to keep from touching himself. He could barely push back into Sebastian's thrusts with how firmly Sebastian held his hips. Completely dependent on Sebastian's cock moving in him, gliding across his prostate. Brad made high-pitched kitten noises with each stroke.

It lasted forever, and just when Brad was starting to wonder if he was going to come or die, Sebastian sped up. He dug in hard with his fingers, shoving himself as far into Brad as he could. Then Sebastian pulsed inside him and choked, "Come now, Bradley."

So Brad did. His orgasm rolled over him like water, completely filling him. The muscles behind his balls contracted. Slow and strong, a liquid explosion of warmth and a happy tingle unfolding inside him, not so much making him come as *releasing* him. He shook uncontrollably and cried out Sebastian's name.

When the shudders faded, Sebastian collapsed to Brad's side, pulling him along. Spooning Brad and still hard inside him.

"Jesus. That might have actually worked," Brad croaked minutes later when he felt up to forming sentences. He was lying on his stomach now, with Sebastian's arm heavy on his back. He turned his head to look at Sebastian's face.

"Huh?" Sebastian mumbled, facing Brad, eyes closed.

"Maybe I feel less guilty."

Sebastian roused himself a little and opened his eyes. "You didn't think it *would* work?"

"Not really."

"Then why did you suggest it?"

Good thing he was so relaxed, or he might be getting embarrassed. "I wanted it."

Sebastian's playful smile crept over his face, this time with a sinful edge. The wicked priest. "Mmm." He pulled himself a little closer and threw his leg over the backs of Brad's thighs. "Yeah?"

"Yeah." Sebastian's closed his eyes, but Brad wasn't done talking. "You ever done anything like that before?"

Sebastian's eyes opened again. "Like what? Punished someone?"

Brad squirmed a little. "Like, um, dominated someone."

Sebastian took a few seconds to answer. "Yeah. Not planned out like that, but yeah. It wasn't the way it is with you, though."

"How is it with me?" Brad asked softly.

"Insanely hot. I thought I was going to pass out."

Brad smiled. He was pretty drowsy, too. He could barely move.

"I spent most of the day thinking about your 'punishment.'" Sebastian grinned. "I had to jerk off at lunchtime, it was making me so nuts."

"Mmm." The idea of Sebastian stroking himself was hot, but he was too tired to do anything about it. "I like that. I'd like to see that sometime."

Sebastian kissed Brad's temple. "Yeah? Maybe next time you need to be punished, I'll tie you to the bed and make you watch while I come all over you."

Brad's eyes popped open as he jerked his head off the bed.

"You tired?" Sebastian asked him, the smile breaking out on his face. Brad's heart started beating in his ears.

"Not that tired," Brad said.

Chapter 27

Sebastian had to go to the State University library in the morning to do research, so he dropped Brad off a block or so from the frat. Brad hadn't had to ask him to do that; he just stopped the car out of sight of the house.

Brad was grateful. Because, while he fully intended to come out? He wanted to be in control of how and when.

It didn't stop him from leaning over to kiss Sebastian, though. They parked under a huge chestnut tree, and no one was around this early on a Saturday. The limbs of the tree came down like a big umbrella, practically touching the street in places. Kissing Sebastian was worth the risk.

"Mmm," Sebastian said, palming Brad's head. "You coming over tonight?"

"Oh, yeah." Brad smiled, and Sebastian leaned in for one more kiss.

"I'll miss you, honey," Sebastian whispered against his lips.

Really, one more quick kiss wouldn't hurt, right?

When Brad finally forced himself to scoot back and grab the door handle, his lips were tingling. Sebastian was looking over at him, smiling, but then turned his focus to something outside Brad's window. "Oh, shit." He looked back at Brad quickly, paling.

Brad closed his eyes. "Okay. Just tell me who it is and how many there are."

"It's Kyle."

Brad slumped in relief. Kyle he could handle.

"I'm sorry, hon," Sebastian said. "You want me to come with you to talk to him? He's waiting for you."

"No, it's all right." Brad leaned back over to kiss Sebastian quickly, just to show him how all right it was. Sebastian looked a little less troubled when Brad pulled away. "It'll be fine. I'll see you later."

"Sure?"

"Sure."

Brad got out, finally. Kyle was standing on the sidewalk under the chestnut tree less than five feet from the car, but Brad didn't say anything until Sebastian had driven away.

He still didn't say anything. Until, finally, Kyle nearly shouted, "*That's* why you worked so hard on those history papers?"

Brad blinked. Not what he'd expected. "Uh, yeah. I guess." Sebastian didn't even grade his papers anymore. He'd said it was a conflict of interest.

"What, that didn't work, so now you're messing around with him for a good grade?"

That was more along the lines of what Brad had expected. He gritted his teeth. "He's my boyfriend."

Kyle blinked, mouth working for a few seconds, then said, "You don't have to do this, man. I'd have helped you with the class if you wanted; you only had to ask—"

"Kyle. Shut the fuck up." Sometimes the guy could be a little thick. "I'm gay. I like cock. I'm not with Sebastian for a grade, I'm with him because I *like* him. Really, really like him."

Kyle's mouth worked some more. "But . . . but those girls . . . all of 'em. I don't . . . Did he *make* you gay?"

"Dude, I will kick your ass if you make one more comment like that about Sebastian. Just—" Brad sighed. *Shit*, he didn't want to do it this way. "It's like having a girlfriend, okay? You don't talk shit about Tank's girlfriend, right? Because Tank is very touchy about his girlfriend."

Kyle nodded, mouth still hanging open.

"It's like that. I am very touchy about my boyfriend. And before you say anything stupid, if you even *imply* that Sebastian is like a girl, in any way, there will be blood. Okay?"

Brad stared at Kyle a few seconds before he finally started nodding. He looked like maybe the shock was getting to him. "Oh. Okay."

"Okay. C'mon, let's get you back to the frat before you faint." Brad sighed and turned toward the house.

"Good idea," Kyle said weakly, still nodding. Brad had to tug on his arm before he moved, though.

Brad got Kyle to the frat and up the front stairs. When he opened the door, Julian was standing in the entry again. Why was he always there?

Jules looked at them, then looked at Kyle more closely. His brow wrinkled. "What's wrong with you?"

"Uh," Kyle said.

"Got overheated," Brad said.

Jules' brow wrinkles grew. "It's, like, fifty-five degrees out there."

"He was in the sauna."

"I thought he was just going to get some gum."

"He decided to take a sauna while he chewed it." Brad was steadily working his way around Jules, pushing Kyle toward the stairs.

"That's just weird," Jules muttered. Then he pulled a feather duster out of his back pocket and started knocking dust off the tops of the many framed pictures of past and present frat members.

Jules was just weird. Brad prodded Kyle up the stairs and forgot all about Jules, thinking instead about the best way to get Kyle to snap out of the shock and make sure he kept his fucking mouth shut until Brad was prepared for his queerness to be general knowledge.

"Brad's gay," Kyle blurted as soon as they walked into their room and found Collin there, a pile of clean laundry on his bed in front of him.

"Kyle!" Brad yelled.

"You told him?" Collin asked at the same time.

"He saw me with Sebastian."

"Collin knows?" Kyle asked. "You told him before you told me?"

Brad scowled at him. He might have had more sympathy if Kyle hadn't just tried to tell Collin himself.

"I found out kinda like you did," Collin told his laundry. "By accident."

"I need to sit down." Kyle stumbled over to his desk chair.

Brad followed and stood over him. "Dude, you *cannot* go around telling people. I'm going to tell the rest of the guys—"

"You are?" Collin asked sharply.

"I'm going to tell the rest of the guys about me." Subtle emphasis on "me." He turned back to Kyle. "But I'm doing it when I'm ready. I'm not fucking having you wandering around telling everyone."

"Dude." Kyle sounded even more hurt. "I wouldn't do that to you, bud. I'd never tell."

"You just walked in here and announced it to Collin!"

Kyle looked confused. "Oh, yeah. I think it was the shock," he said slowly. "Won't happen again, swear."

Brad eyed him for a minute while Kyle looked up at him in earnest. "It can't. If I don't control how this comes out, it could get ugly."

Some kind of understanding settled over Kyle. He nodded firmly and sat up straighter.

It still took Kyle forever to get his mind around it. At least, it seemed like forever. Brad sat in his desk chair and listened to Kyle's random thoughts on his gayness. They bubbled up out of the guy like gas out of a tar pit.

Brad was annoyed and bored as shit within ten minutes.

Apparently, Collin was, too. "It's not like he's the only gay guy in the frat," Collin told Kyle scornfully.

Kyle stared at him. "There are other gay guys in this frat?"

Collin shrugged and looked away, still folding laundry. Kyle stared at him a minute longer, then turned to Brad, eyes wide and face slack in surprise. "Are there? Other gay guys in this frat?"

Brad shrugged, managing a much less self-conscious one than Collin. "Statistically there have to be, man."

"Yeah, but do you *know* any?"

Collin froze with a pair of holey briefs in his hand and whipped his head around. Kyle didn't notice, focused solely on Brad. Brad finally dropped his hands from behind his head and gave Kyle his most forbidding look. "I don't come and tell, dude."

"You *fucked* him? This other gay guy?" Kyle's voice rose so high Brad thought it might crack.

Shit. "Why are you hets all so intercourse-centric? There's a lot more to sex than sticking it in and wiggling it around."

Kyle's mouth dropped open. Brad felt like he was forcefully broadening Kyle's mind with, like, a can opener. But at least Collin had relaxed, sitting on his bed and looking at Brad with amused interest.

"*Hets*? Intercourse-centric? Who *are* you?"

"Same guy I've always been. This is just a part of me you've never seen before." He crossed his arms over his chest and eyed Kyle steadily.

Kyle didn't seem to notice; he was staring off into space. He shut his mouth with a snap and swallowed audibly. "Okay. Okay, so, there's hand jobs and blowjobs and fucking, right?"

Brad snorted. "That's a good start."

"What else is there?"

Brad tilted his chair back. He never got to be the tutor, so he planned to make the most of it. "Well, there's frottage. Or, as the French say it, 'frot-AZH.' A lot of guys start there." He supposed. Based on his research.

Collin smirked. Kyle's eyes widened. "Frottage?"

"Rubbing off on someone. It's really great when one guy has his hand around both—"

"Dude!" Kyle shouted, palm to Brad and doing the closed-eyed cringe. "No details. Only the basics, man." Collin started coughing hysterically into the pair of socks he'd just balled up. Kyle looked at him. "Got to you, too, huh dude?"

Collin coughed harder and turned away. Kyle's brow pulled together. "I think you made him inhale something, man. That was cruel." He shook his head slowly.

Brad grinned. "He'll be all right."

Once Collin had recovered himself, Kyle broached the subject again. "So, uh. That's it, right?"

Brad smiled even more broadly. "You know, your asshole—"

"Don'tusethatword!" Kyle was doing a whole-body cringe this time. Brad chanced a look at Collin, who was desperately trying not to laugh and refusing to meet Brad's eyes.

Brad got his smile under control and cleared his throat. "Sorry. You know, your *anus* . . ." he paused to see if Kyle had any objections. Kyle made a pained "go ahead" motion with his hand. "Your anus is one of the most sensitive parts of your body. It's more sensitive than a lot of your dick. 'Course, if you'd never been circumcised and still had a frenulum, that wouldn't be the case."

"Dude! How do you know I'm circumcised? Have you been checking me out?" Brad raised an eyebrow and stared at Kyle until Kyle muttered, "Yeah, never mind."

"There are lots of things you can do to your anus—or someone else can do—that are pretty fucking awesome. And that's not even mentioning the prostate."

"Oh, God," Kyle whined. He planted his elbows on his knees and hid his face in his hands.

Some devil made him do it. Brad smiled big and winked at Collin before saying, "And of course, there's getting fucked."

Kyle's hands fisted in his hair. "But you don't do that, right?"

Brad just sat there, the chair creaking as he rocked it back and forth on its hind legs. Collin stared at him. Kyle froze.

Collin cleared his throat. "You *bottom*?"

Brad nodded precisely. "All the time." Enunciating. He didn't know why he wanted these guys to know. Well, he did. It pissed him off for some reason that they would just figure, since he was the jock and Sebastian was the brain, that Brad must be fucking him.

Even fucking *Collin* thought so, Brad could tell by the way his eyes bugged out.

Kyle lifted his head and looked at Collin. "Did he say what I think he just said?" he asked faintly.

Collin stared at Brad, but answered Kyle. "Yeah. He did. Um . . . excuse me, I think I need to go take a shower." He grabbed a clean pair of briefs and a T-shirt off the bed and scrambled out the door, holding his clothes in front of his groin.

Kyle looked at Brad reproachfully. "Dude. You can't say shit like that to just *anyone*. You scared the hell out of Collin. I'm your best friend; I can come to terms with this shit—" Kyle cleared his throat "—given time. But Collin, man, and the other guys . . ." Kyle shook his head.

That was enough bullshit for one day. "Kyle, I don't really give a fuck anymore. I'm not hiding it, and if the other guys want to kick me out of the frat, they can go right ahead. After *I* tell them." He let the front legs of his chair hit the floor and stood up. "And just so we're clear, *Sebastian's* my best friend."

Kyle just stared while Brad grabbed his cell and his keys off his desk and checked his backpack to make sure it had his books. He slung the strap over his shoulder, smiled perfunctorily at Kyle, clapped him on the shoulder, and walked out. "Going to the library. See ya."

Chapter 28

Brad didn't go to the library. He hiked out to the organic garden plot on the edge of campus and weeded peas. It was coolish, but warm enough that he had to take off his sweatshirt. The sun kept breaking through the clouds, and the ground was soft for weeding.

For the first hour or so, he was the only one there, but then Professor Harris came out to check on something. When Brad waved at her, she left the greenhouse to talk to him.

"Hi Brad." She smiled. She always smiled.

"Hey, Professor Harris."

She huffed softly at him. "How many times have I asked you to call me Helen? We shovel manure together once a week, you can call me by my first name."

He shrugged and kept hacking at weeds. She smiled again; he could feel it in the air. She changed the subject, though. "What are you doing this summer?"

"Um, I don't know." He stopped and leaned on his hoe. "Guess I'll move home and get a job." What was Sebastian doing this summer? If he stayed here, Brad could see him sometimes, but if Sebastian went home to Colorado . . .

Sebastian hadn't said anything to him. Or asked Brad what he was doing over the summer.

"How about you stay here and work for me?"

Brad focused on her, startled. "What?"

"It doesn't pay very much, but I need an aide for summer term. You'd be taking care of the garden, mostly."

Brad looked around. It was an acre, at least. It would keep him pretty freaking busy. "Don't you have to be a grad student to be an aide?"

She huffed again. "Family Sciences doesn't have grad students. I get to pick the upperclassman I like the most and who I know will work hard." She smiled even wider at him. "And you get to keep a lot of the produce. I'll even let you take the Master Preserver Certification class for free."

"Seriously?" Brad's heart leapt. Call him weird, but he loved to pickle vegetables and can sauce. If he were a master preserver, he could do tons of stuff. He could teach community ed classes in food preservation. He could even sell his sauces at farmers' markets if he wanted.

Which he hadn't actually been aware he wanted to do, but right now he wanted it so bad he could taste it. It tasted like the perfect combination of vinegar, dill, garlic, and spices. Oh, yeah, and he could work on that pickling spice blend he'd started to perfect last summer in his mom's kitchen. It had almost no allspice, because Brad thought it was too overpowering, so he—

"Brad?"

"Huh?"

"So, whadaya think?"

"Oh hell yeah. I'll do it, Helen."

ΘΛΓ

Brad didn't tell Sebastian he was going to be on campus over the summer when he went over that night. He was waiting for the right time. They watched some dumb movie after Paul and Toby had left, but it was really just an excuse to lie on the couch and make out. Which led to other things, of course.

Sunday morning didn't seem to be the right time, either.

Or Monday or Wednesday, when Brad showed up all sweaty. There seemed to be a direct relationship between how sweaty he was when he showed up and how fast they got it on.

Friday morning Brad couldn't wait anymore; he needed to get it out. Sebastian might not even care, but . . . Brad cut his run short and headed over to Sebastian's early. He was standing at the bottom of the stairs to Sebastian's door, sweaty, hands on hips, letting his breath slow down—working up his nerve—when he heard the door open.

"Hey! I must be late," Toby's voice drifted down from the top of the stairs. When Brad looked, he could just make him out in the shadows up there. "Is it the Frat Boy and Toppy hour already?" Toby walked down the stairs, smiling at Brad.

"Hey, Toby. I'm early." Toby's eyes held a smirk when he said it, but he refrained from commenting on Brad's eagerness.

"Didn't think I was late. But Paul's gonna be if he doesn't hurry up." Translation: beware of attack roommate.

"Oh, goody. Frat Boy's here." Paul's nasty voice. Right on cue. Lovely. Brad closed his eyes, pinching the bridge of his nose. "Your master is on the phone with his sister," Paul snarked, coming down the stairs.

Toby rolled his eyes and said to Brad in a much nicer voice, "Just go on up. He's about to get off."

"Oh, we all know that's the truth," Paul said sweetly.

Brad gritted his teeth and didn't punch him. Paul must have seen it in his face, though, because he shut up and marched off.

"Sorry," Toby said. "I've had about enough of him, so I guess you're way past that, huh?"

"Yeah."

Toby clapped him on the shoulder. "Just go up, dude."

When Brad walked in the door, Sebastian had the phone in his hand, but he'd obviously just hung up. "Hey, honey!" Sebastian said, smiled broadly and walking over to Brad, looking up those couple inches into Brad's eyes.

Brad chickened out again. He knew what the problem was: he was scared Sebastian wouldn't care. When Sebastian brought his head down, Brad let him because then he didn't have to say anything and find out how Sebastian really felt.

He attempted to man up, though, while Sebastian kissed him, walking him from the door to the couch. He tried to get himself to stop everything and tell Sebastian. It wasn't even that big a deal, right? Just, *Oh, hey, I got a job on campus this summer.*

He could have said it without interrupting anything while Sebastian was yanking off their clothes, or at least the necessary ones. Or when Sebastian pushed him down on the couch and just stood looking at him for a few seconds.

It might have stopped their momentum, though. Then they wouldn't be grinding naked against each other now, sealed together from lips to hips. Sebastian's hard cock against Brad's belly, Brad's against his thigh. Now Brad was fighting *not* to say something.

Like, "I love you." Because he really didn't want to know Sebastian's reaction to that. And he really didn't want to say it like this, during sex, when Sebastian could blame it on the moment and ignore it.

When he came, shooting against Sebastian's skin and tangling in his wet leg hairs, shouting wordlessly to keep from saying the wrong thing, he realized where his priorities lay. What he needed to say to Sebastian first. Because he might not want to know what Sebastian thought about how he felt, but he needed to know.

Sebastian fell on him, and Brad held him even though his muscles felt too weak. Long after their breathing had returned to normal, Sebastian was stroking his hair, naked chest against Brad's, cum gluing them together.

Sebastian kissed Brad's temple. Brad held him tighter and stroked his hand up and down Sebastian's back. Shut his eyes and just felt the happy stuff for now. He needed to hang on to this a while longer.

Eventually they had to move. They took a shower, all steam and hands stroking and petting, cleaning each other silently. Brad wrapped Sebastian in his arms and held him for a long time, standing in the spray.

They had a while before Brad had to leave, and they ended up in bed, cuddling, half-dressed.

Chapter 29

Sebastian leaned over the side of the bed, looking for some socks. He heard Brad rustle around, sit up against the headboard. Then Brad took his hand, and he stopped and rolled to face him.

"Should I come back tonight?"

"Yeah. Of course." Brad looked apprehensive. "I want you to, honey." Sebastian squeezed his hand.

"Tonight's the last rush party, but I can skip it. But tomorrow night we induct the new pledges, and all the brothers should be there."

Sebastian reached up for a quick kiss, then leaned over the side of the bed again, taking his hand back. He'd had the damn socks earlier; where did they go? "Probably better, really, hon. I was running out of numbers to bribe Paul with. He's got plans tonight, though."

"Huh?"

Damn it. "I've been bribing Paul with the numbers of guys I've met to keep quiet about you." His heart beat a little harder, annoyed with him for letting that slip.

Brad moved around again. "You have?"

Sebastian couldn't read anything in his tone. "Is that all right?" he asked softly, turning to see him again. Brad looked at him a moment. He rolled onto his back when Brad didn't answer right away.

Brad played with the sheet on his lap instead. "I know you've been with a lot of guys, Sebastian."

"Yeah?" Sebastian asked carefully. Somehow, a lot of those guys seemed pretty colorless now. Hell, all of them.

"I mean, I heard rumors." Brad shrugged and met Sebastian's eyes "I guess some of it could just be talk, like with me and girls."

Why did Sebastian want to wrap Brad up in his arms and kiss him until he smiled whenever he got all insecure like this? It was a mystery. "I think I've probably been with a lot more guys than you have girls." He flinched when he said it, but he couldn't lie to Brad.

"Yeah." Brad let out a disgusted-sounding breath. "But I probably lied to more girls than you have guys."

"It's easier with guys, hon. For one thing, you can just tell them you aren't looking for anything serious. If they don't want to play, they don't. Most of the time. Besides, the ones you meet in bars tend to be looking for a lot of the same thing."

"So . . . when we met, were you looking for a relationship?"

Sebastian smiled at him, because Brad just made him smile. He reached up and brought Brad's face around. "No, hon. But I found one." Strange, but true.

Brad smiled suddenly, and it was mesmerizing. Like watching the sun come back again after a solar eclipse.

Chapter 30

On Saturday morning, Brad woke up early and watched Sebastian sleep. He knew it was dorky and he tried to stop, but he couldn't seem to look away. He'd done it last Saturday, too.

He was lucky. Really fucking lucky. He wanted to just stay here forever. But he had to get back to his room and do some laundry, as well as inventory the damned kitchen at the frat house and get ready for the stupid pledge ceremony.

He sighed. He'd rather be here with his boyfriend. Who seemed to be waking up. Just before he thought Sebastian was going to open his eyes, he rolled over and scooted backward into Sebastian's body. He didn't want to get caught staring at the shape of Sebastian's jaw or his long eyelashes in the sunlight, but he could rub up on him some.

"Hey, honey." Sebastian's voice was hoarse. He yawned and stretched, then dropped an arm over Brad's waist and pulled him in tight.

Brad smiled his by now customary goofy grin, looking out the window. "Morning." He laced his fingers through Sebastian's and brought his hand up to kiss it. He could feel Sebastian smiling into the back of his neck, then his lips when he kissed Brad on the shoulder.

They just lay around a while, Sebastian talking about his dissertation again. In spite of the fact that Brad had no clue what a Cycladic frying pan was—except for it not being a cooking implement—or why Sebastian's theory that they were sacred musical instruments was so controversial, he loved listening to Sebastian talk about it. Sebastian didn't seem to care that Brad wasn't as smart as him, either.

After a while, Sebastian talked himself out, and they just cuddled, drowsing. Shifting around some, but always touching. Brad loved this. Lying here with Sebastian, he always felt so happy his skin probably glowed. Melting into Sebastian's.

Sebastian's hand on Brad's back was soothing. Occasionally sweeping across or down or just taking a lazy trip around, palm pressed against Brad's skin. Sebastian rose up on one elbow, propping his head on his hand, but not like he wanted Brad's attention. He was just there, looking out the window. It was a beautiful day. Starting to cloud up, but nice enough now. The kind of day you wanted to go out and take a walk before it rained, stroll along with your boyfriend's hand in yours.

He had the strangest urges lately.

"Sebastian?"

"Yeah, hon?" Sebastian leaned down and kissed his temple, still staring out the window, lost in some kind of thought. About ancient pottery, probably. Brad rolled over onto his back, tucking himself almost under Sebastian's scruffy chin. He stretched up to press his lips against Sebastian's jawbone where it curved out and defined the underside of his face.

"What if I never come out? Will you dump me?"

Sebastian looked down at him sharply. His eyes were so brown. He leaned forward again and kissed his lips. "I don't really want to answer that, Brad."

"I wanna know."

Sebastian was silent a long time, his eyes flickering around Brad's face. He sighed. "Not right away. It'd probably take a while before I got sick of being your shameful secret." The teasing smile flitted across his face, but didn't seem to want to hang around.

"How long is a while?" Brad said to the underside of Sebastian's chin, and to his whiskers. He let his eyes roam down Sebastian's neck.

"Bradley, hon," Sebastian sighed, stroking Brad's short hair back from his forehead with the flat of his hand. He cupped Brad's cheek. "I like you. A lot. *A lot*, a lot. I'd probably stick it out longer than I should, months for sure. But the minute the pain outweighs the fun? I'm gone, honey."

Brad swallowed. "Is that all I am? Fun?"

"Hon, you're lots of things for me."

Brad stared at the wall across from the foot of the bed. It was blank. Just a white wall with nothing on it. Wasn't like he was really seeing it, anyway. Could you listen with your eyes? 'Cause that's what he was doing, maybe.

"No, hon. You're so much more than fun."

Brad let out a slow breath. Sebastian wouldn't lie to him. But . . . "There's probably a better deal out there for you than me. Someone who's out."

"I don't want a better deal." Brad turned back to Sebastian. He was smiling and his eyes had gone all liquid. Melted chocolate. He leaned in and kissed Brad, lips clinging, pulling away slowly. "'Not right now. Maybe not for a long time."

Brad's heart started pounding away in his chest, sudden and loud in his ears. "You know I'm in love with you, right?"

Slowly, Sebastian lost his smile. He smoothed his thumb across Brad's temple, looking very, very serious. "Yeah. I had pretty much figured that out."

Brad's heart clenched up a split second, even though he'd been sure he didn't need to hear Sebastian say it back. He cleared his throat, tried to work up saliva. "Is . . . that all right?" He couldn't seem to look away from Sebastian's eyes, even though he was damn sure he didn't want to watch Sebastian say no.

Sebastian stroked back his hair one more time. "Yeah, hon. That's all right. Better than."

Thank God. That was all he needed from Sebastian for now.

Sebastian's kiss was perfect. Starting out slow but quickly getting aggressive, hot and desperate, Sebastian pressing his body to Brad's then lifting himself over him, grinding him into the bed, thrusting short and sharp into the furrow between his hip and pelvis.

Brad scrambled to get the blankets out of the way enough to feel skin against him, but he barely made it before he was coming, crying into Sebastian's mouth, letting Sebastian take it in. Everything got slippery and then slipperier when Sebastian came, too.

Five minutes after telling Sebastian he loved him, Brad was drifting in a post-coital haze, and he never wanted to come out of it.

He eventually did float out of the haze when Sebastian pulled him into the shower. Sebastian stood behind Brad, soaping him up, when he said softly, "Don't do it for me, hon. Do it for yourself."

"I know," Brad said, trying to swallow the sharp pain in his chest.

Sebastian went on—something Brad had been desperately hoping he wouldn't do. "What if we break up? You might regret coming out because of me."

Brad stepped forward, Sebastian's hands slipping off of him. He started to rinse himself clean. "I'm gay. I told you."

Sebastian stepped up behind him, circling his waist loosely. "I don't want to be the reason you come out."

"You wouldn't be." His voice wasn't as strong as he wanted it to be. "Not the only reason."

"Honey," Sebastian murmured. "I need to be sure after what you just said in the bedroom, yeah?"

Brad swallowed, wondering why he wasn't mad. *You should have known he wasn't taking you seriously.* Tears prickled behind his eyes. He didn't wait for Sebastian to say any more and make it worse, just stepped out of his arms and right out of the shower, grabbing a towel on his way out of the room. He needed to get out of here so he could breathe. He found his clothes on the floor of Sebastian's bedroom, and he was trying to zip his jeans when Sebastian appeared in the doorway.

"Honey, c'mon, please. Just think about it, yeah?"

"I am thinking about it." Brad couldn't see his fingers; they were all blurry. He could feel his zipper though, sort of. He finally got the fucking thing up and dropped to the floor to pull on his shoes.

"Brad," Sebastian said, voice rising. "I'm not saying I want to break up with you. I already told you I'm okay with how you feel—"

Oh. There was the mad. "*Okay* with it? You're okay with me acting like a fool for you? Being in love with you when you don't give a shit about me? When you don't even take me being gay seriously?" He stared up at Sebastian a second before yanking on his shoes. Fuck the laces.

"That's not fair, Brad! You *know* I care about you, I—"

Brad stood up. He had to go past Sebastian to get to the front door.

"Brad!" Sebastian's voice followed him down the hall. "We need to talk about this. I don't even know what being in love *is*. Maybe—"

Brad stopped and turned back to Sebastian. "I've known what being in love is since I came home with you that night," he said, suddenly very steady and calm. Sebastian's jaw worked, but he was speechless. "I never asked for anything from you. I didn't need you to say it back. I just needed you to believe me and maybe, I don't know, be okay with how I feel. I need to just . . . I need to go to the fucking library."

He waited for a response, but Sebastian just stared at him with those chocolate eyes. For a second, Brad wanted to walk back and let Sebastian hold him, maybe even cry, because he had a feeling these weren't angry tears balling up at the base of his skull.

Instead he turned and walked out, and Sebastian let him.

Chapter 31

Brad hiked out to the organic garden plot on the edge of campus and weeded peas again.

Well, more like he sat in the dirt between rows and let the big ball of unshed tears and the slicing pain in his head and throat eat at him. Take up residence in the bones in his face, making his cheeks and skull ache.

The sky was gray with clouds now, maybe in sympathy. A southwesterly wind was whipping at him, and he was all by himself. In the garden, but also everywhere else, right? This was exactly what he'd known would happen. He didn't deserve to be in love. Or maybe he deserved to be in love with someone who didn't want him to be.

Because he'd been such a jerk to all those girls before.

Because Sebastian probably didn't want someone who wasn't as smart as he was. Brad couldn't even remember what an amphora was.

Because he wasn't the right guy for Sebastian. He was just some naive, inexperienced kid who'd fallen in love with the guy who'd taken his virginity.

He was doomed to a life of pain and solitude.

You're being a drama queen.

Brad ignored the little voice in his heart. It seemed best.

You overreacted.

But he made me love him! So much for ignoring the voice.

You could have talked to him.

What if he really can't *love me? Isn't he just supposed to* know, *like I know I love him?*

His heart didn't seem to have any answers for that. That showed the smug bastard organ. He wrapped his arms around his knees and rested his forehead on his clasped hands, watching tears hit the dirt between his feet. If he had to cry out the ache in his chest, he probably needed to start, because it looked like a monumental job.

Unfortunately, he didn't seem capable of endurance crying. When his tears dried up, the ache in his chest was pretty much the same.

To make matters worse, he started thinking again.

The day he'd admitted to himself he was gay was the day he'd started to feel really real. He'd known since then that he was going to come out to the world. His family—done—the frat, all his exes, people in general. Why would Sebastian think Brad would only come out for him?

Maybe because you've done and been what others expected you to be your whole life.

Goddammit. The little voice was back.

You wouldn't even admit you're gay to yourself because it didn't fit others' image of you.

Oh God. Make the little voice stop being right.

You're majoring in PE because everyone assumed you would. You don't even like football that much. Not playing it.

He didn't want to get dragged into arguing with the little voice again. The bastard always won, but this time Brad had him. *I'm minoring in home ec. I'm in charge of the frat kitchen. I did eventually admit I'm gay.*

Glimmers of light in the dark.

Do you have to get all melodramatic about it?

Hellooooo! This is your inner drama queen speaking! I'm you, you asshole. You're *melodramatic. You think I liked being trapped in here since we were fourteen?*

Hey, you called me a drama queen earlier!

No, that was you.

That took a minute to puzzle out, and by then Brad was seeing the truth of the whole argument. Except maybe the drama queen part.

Okay . . . so it was time to just do it. Suck it up, stand up and tell the frat tonight and the world tomorrow. All those girls he'd used.

Uh, yeah.

Suddenly the conviction was there. He was going to do it. He'd tell the frat at the meeting. Then he needed to talk to Sebastian. Brad wasn't giving up that easy ever again.

First step: set up his support network.

Chapter 32

When the door clicked shut behind Brad, Sebastian stared at the carpet, bewildered, something weighing down his chest. It was kind of an ache. He sat down where he stood, in his bedroom doorway. *What the actual fuck just happened here?*

He could still see the look on Brad's face when Brad had asked if it was all right to be in love with him. The ache in his chest twanged, like something had plucked its string. That look had changed *everything*, hadn't it? Instead of letting Brad down gently, like Sebastian had meant to—because he'd seen this coming, of course—he hadn't. Hadn't said any of the things he'd planned to say. Nothing about infatuation and being Brad's first. No bittersweet achiness because he knew things were going to end and the fun would be over.

He'd even told Brad it was okay—and how fair was that to Brad? He'd let Brad think there might be more to this than stellar sex and close friendship. He'd hurt Brad.

And now the fun was over, anyway.

That's what the weight in his chest must be. Knowing how much damage he'd caused. Letting Brad think he might be in love with him, when he wasn't. If he *was* in love with Brad, he'd know it, right? Didn't love come with little tweeting cartoon birds flying around? Okay, yeah, well not that, but something that made it obvious and unmistakable. He didn't know anything for sure, so it must not be love. All he knew was that he'd made Brad sad. Worse than sad.

Heartbroken.

In this moment, if Sebastian thought he could make it work, he would have carved his own heart out with a butter knife and offered it to Brad. Not because he was in love; just as a sort of replacement heart. An emotional transplant. Then he could have the broken heart and Brad could feel better. He could handle the broken heart. It couldn't hurt any worse than this did right now.

He'd *hurt* Brad.

He was an asshole.

Ergo, he needed a beer.

Chapter 33

B rad rang the doorbell at Ashley's sorority. No one answered within ten seconds—which was just too damn long for a reasonable person to wait—so he pounded on it to get someone's attention.

Some young-looking girl swung the door back forcefully, shouting, "Just a— Oh, hi. Brad Feller, right?" She blinked rapidly at him.

"Yeah, hi. Is Ashley here?"

The girl stopped blinking. "Yeah, come on in, I guess." Brad followed her fuzzy dinosaur slippers into the entry hall. "Wait here." She turned toward the stairway and screeched, "Ashley! You have a visitor in the foyer!"

She turned back to Brad. "You know, she just got home from spending the night at her boyfriend's frat."

He hadn't even thought of that. He might have caught her if he'd gone straight back to his own frat.

"Brittany, give it up. He's off the market." Ashley's voice. She was walking down the stairs, smiling at him. It looked genuine. "Hey, Brad. What's up?"

"I need your help," he said quickly, stepping forward. "I decided I'm going to come—"

"Brad! Not here, sweetie. How about you meet me—"

"At the coffee shop? Okay. I'll get you a coffee, light cream."

Ashley blinked. "Um, I'll just walk over with you, okay? I can get my own coffee."

They didn't talk on the way. Brad kept trying to, but Ashley kept telling him to wait. At the coffee shop, she found them a secluded corner.

"Brad, stay here," she said. "I'm going to get a coffee. Don't talk to *anyone*. Do you understand me?"

What was she so worked up about? "Okay." He nodded. Because that's what he did here: he listened to Ashley and nodded.

When she came back, she sat down and leaned across the table to him. "Okay, so you're going to come out?" she asked, barely loud enough to hear.

Brad blinked a few times. "How did you know that?"

Ashley rolled her eyes. "Because you practically told my whole sorority by almost slipping in front of Brattany, and sweetie, that ain't the way you need to do it. This is all about information control."

"I thought her name was Brittany."

"Only to her face. It's Brattany everywhere else. Now, are you going to do this at the meeting tonight?"

"Yeah." This wasn't going quite the way he'd expected. "I was thinking when all the brothers are there, but before the new pledges come in."

"Okay, good. We'll get Kyle and Collin in on this, too, but first you and I are going to come up with a plan. It's going to spread faster than you can run. You can't control how people are going to find out or what they're going to say. We need to figure out what spin we're going to put on this and how."

"You sound like my PR consultant."

"Oh, sweetie, that's what I am. Didn't you know I'm a marketing major? I wonder if I can get extra credit for this."

"God, I was the lamest boyfriend, ever, wasn't I?"

Ashley shrugged. "I've had worse."

"I was. I don't know how you like your coffee, I didn't know your major, I wouldn't have sex with you. That's only the beginning. And it wasn't just you. All those girls deserve to hear it from me, personally."

"That's impossible. And certainly not all of them."

"Okay, so which ones would deserve to hear it from me?"

"It depends, but Brad—"

"On what?"

"On how serious it was." Ashley sighed. "Okay, I guess we're going to talk about this?"

He nodded.

"If it was just some girl you dated once? Or only a few times? She can hear it through the grapevine. Same with some girl you just hooked up with at a party or something. Are all those rumors true?"

"No, thank God," Brad breathed. "But some are."

"Only the more serious 'relationships.'" She did that air quotes thing with her fingers, making him wince.

"Shit. I wasn't serious about *any* of them," he admitted, but she just shrugged and made an "it is what it is" kind of face.

"All right. Do it this way: if you refer to her as your 'ex' in your head or to other people? You have to tell her in person."

Shit. Brad closed his eyes and started to compose a mental list.

"You know, they're going to be upset. I'd be mad if I felt like some guy used me for cover or something. Led me on. I *was* mad."

"I didn't *know* I was leading them on."

Ashley snorted. "You just try that line and see if it works with them better than it did with me."

"Great," he muttered.

Ashley lay one hand over his, startling him. "It's going to be okay. Sebastian will help you get through this."

Oh, God. Tears again. They just snuck up on you, didn't they?

"Oh, no. You guys broke up?"

He bit his lip and looked at the wall. He couldn't deal with rehashing this.

"You just have to be macho even when you're gay, don't you?" Ashley sighed. "You're coming out anyway?"

"Of course I am!"

"Shhh. Sorry. That was insensitive. Of course you are. You're still gay, after all."

"That's what I'm saying!"

She hushed him again. He glanced around. Okay, a few people had looked.

"We'll just deal with the frat tonight. By tomorrow morning, I'll have let something leak that puts a positive spin on this. Brattany has her uses. And then . . . you have a plan for getting Sebastian back?"

Brad nodded. "Not giving up."

"Good." She finally let go of his hand, apparently because she needed hers back. She pulled a pen out of her purse. "Now, what exact words were you planning on using when you come out tonight?"

"Uh . . ."

It didn't really matter that Brad didn't know. She told him what to say, how to stand, when to blink. She even told him what he was going to say to Collin and Kyle, then made suggestions for planned responses to the stupidest questions he could imagine getting. By the time they were done, she had an outline for him on her java jacket, and a stack of napkins she referred to as the PR Plan for herself.

It made Brad's head spin.

Right before he left, Ashley leaned across the table and grabbed his forearm. "Probably lots of the girls you were with used you as much as you did them. I did."

"You did? For what?"

"People know who you are. You're one of the better ball players here, and you're the kind of person people notice."

Brad frowned.

"Just trust me, Brad, 'kay?"

"Doesn't matter if those girls were using me, anyway. What matters is what I did."

"Don't talk yourself into thinking you don't deserve happiness." When had they started talking about happiness? "You spent a lot of years being what everyone else thought you should be. I think you did your time, sweetie, and now you get to be happy."

Brad didn't know what to say. "No one told me I had to be straight."

"Someone did, obviously."

He opened his mouth to deny it, but . . . "Maybe you're right."

Chapter 34

K yle was in their room when Brad got back to the frat. Brad walked in and shut the door firmly behind him.

Ashley seemed to have everything under control, so on the way back Brad had started focusing on Sebastian again. He sort of felt like crying. Again.

He walked over to his bed and threw himself on his back, pressing the heels of his hands into his eyes. Kyle was staring at him, he could feel it.

"What's wrong?"

"What makes you think something's wrong?" His voice bounced back at him from where his forearms blocked his face.

"Uh, you have tearstains on your cheeks."

He dropped his hands and scowled at Kyle. Kyle shrugged. "I'm observant."

Brad bit his lips together, but eventually decided on, "Sebastian and I aren't seeing each other anymore."

Kyle was silent, eyebrows crawling up his forehead. "What happened?" he finally asked.

Brad closed his eyes again. He had no intention of getting into it with Kyle. When "I love him, but he doesn't love me" slipped out of his mouth, he felt as embarrassed as Kyle looked.

This might have been more appropriate to share with Ashley.

"Oh." Kyle's voice was soft. "I'm sorry, man."

Brad shrugged, eyes still closed. "S'okay." It wasn't, of course. But he wasn't going to cry all over Kyle, that was for sure.

"Is that it? The only reason?"

Brad wasn't sure anymore. He cracked his eyes open to squint at the ceiling. "I didn't know if I was ready to come out. Or maybe he didn't think I was ready."

"And he didn't want to be with a guy who wasn't out?"

"That's not exactly it, either." There was something stuck in his throat. "But it doesn't matter, because I'm going to come out. You know," he cleared his throat and flicked a look at Kyle, who seemed attentive, elbows propped on his knees. "He thought I was going to come out just for him, but that's only part of it. It's not even a big part of it. I mean, ever since I figured out I really am gay, I figured I was going to tell people. Sebastian just maybe readjusted my timeline. Is that so bad?"

"No. I don't think so. People do a lot of weird shit for those they love."

Brad fidgeted a minute, and was just about to ask him more when Collin walked in. He stopped in the doorway, obviously sensing something was off, then stepped through and carefully shut the door behind him. "What's up?"

Brad sat up. "I'm coming out to the frat tonight."

"Tonight?" They both spoke at once.

Brad set his jaw again and nodded. "Yeah. Come with me, you guys. We need to plan." He stood. "Oh, and Sebastian and I broke up." He looked carefully into Collin's eyes when he said it. Yeah, he'd told Collin they could see what happened between them, but that was before. He wasn't up to it right now. He couldn't actually imagine being up to it ever.

He might be acting all take-charge and maybe even unemotional, but that wasn't how he felt inside, that was for fucking sure. Inside he felt like wild animals were feasting on his heart.

"C'mon, you two. We've got shit to plan. Oh wait, gotta make sure I have my outline."

Chapter 35

Sebastian was going to miss Brad. Really, it kind of sucked that he wasn't in love with him. It would have been cool to continue seeing him. Those Saturday mornings when they woke up and lay around talking? Those were nice. Better than nice, actually. They made him feel . . . warm inside. Peaceful.

And the way Brad looked at him sometimes from under his brows. Vulnerable and insecure. He didn't look at anyone else like that, Sebastian was certain. That look was just for him. Which was good, because other people might take advantage of Brad. Not protect him and nurture him, like Sebastian did. Not be careful of his feelings.

Oh. Wait. He'd crushed Brad's feelings.

Sebastian slid off the couch and onto the floor, landing hard on his butt.

Assholes like him weren't good enough to sit on the couch.

He needed another beer.

On his way into the kitchen, the phone rang. He stopped and stared. It could only be one person at a time like this. Sophie had a nose for tragedies of the heart.

Chapter 36

Brad, Kyle, and Collin went to the bar around the corner from the bar around the corner to plan. They didn't actually plan much, other than Brad standing up during the "New Business" part of the meeting and proclaiming his gayness. Kyle's eyes glowed with excitement. Collin looked like he wanted to puke. Kyle had to finish his beer for him.

Kyle had gone from confused and possibly hurt to a card-carrying member of PFLAG. Literally; he'd shown Brad the card the other day. When Brad had come into their room after his night class on Wednesday, he caught Kyle frantically trying to hide a book under his pillow. He was pretty convinced it was going to be gay porn.

But once he managed to wrestle it away from Kyle, he saw it was *Brotherhood: Gay Life in College Fraternities*. When Kyle got over Brad holding his head in his armpit, he took his notes out and started babbling about writing a non-discrimination policy and creating something called a Safe Zone.

Kyle seemed to have come to terms with Brad's sexual orientation.

"So," Kyle said excitedly as they were walking back to the frat house. "Have you planned out what you're going to say?"

"Yeah, I'm going to say, 'I'm gay. Deal with it.' And whatever else Ashley wrote down for me to say."

Kyle stopped walking and turned to stare at Brad, mouth hanging open. He looked . . . offended. "That's *it*? This is your chance to really make a statement, dude. The Greek system pays a lot of lip service to equality and acceptance, but they haven't been so great about actually accepting the LGBTQ community, you know."

"I *am* making a statement. I'm telling everyone I like cock." Even Collin, who'd been basically green and silent since they were in the bar, smiled faintly at that.

By then, Kyle had processed the rest of what Brad had said. "Ashley? You mean *my* Ashley? She knows?"

"She didn't tell you that? She knew you knew." They started walking again.

Kyle flushed. "I might have accidentally told her."

Whatever. "She's known longer than either of you have."

"So, you actually have quite a bit of experience with this coming out thing," Kyle said.

"Huh. Guess so. But I didn't plan any of those. My family, Ashley, both you guys; all accidents."

"And Sebastian. You came out to him," Collin pointed out.

Brad stopped walking. Huh. He had.

"Dude, seriously, though. You're missing a golden opportunity to say a few things to the guys."

"Kyle, why don't you write down a few things for *you* to say? Then you can read it to everyone when I'm done." Assuming anyone would be listening to anything at that point.

"Oh," Kyle said. "Yeah. Yeah, I'm gonna do that. That's great, man!" He started walking faster, pulling ahead of them.

"Is there a word for a guy fag hag?" Brad asked.

Collin snorted. "We'll have to make one up."

Chapter 37

A round his fifth beer, Sebastian sighed into the phone. "We've been talking over an hour and a half, Sophie."

"I know. I'm almost sick of it. I never thought I'd experience that."

"You can't be sick of it. I neeeeed you. Fucking with the status quo one night won't hurt us."

"Okay, seriously, how much have you had to drink?"

"Who cares? Just help me figure this out. What's the deal with love? Love hurts, yeah? This doesn't hurt. Didn't hurt. Until I stomped on my little man's heart." He paused to belch. "He's not little. I meant that figuratively."

Sophie snorted. "Love always hurt me. But, Sebastian?"

"Speak, sister."

"Maybe that's not really love."

"It hurt Dad, and he loved Mom."

Sophie went silent. Sebastian found it ominous. "Sophie?"

"I talked to him about it once, when that guy Alec broke up with me. You remember Alec? He was the lead singer of this band—"

"We're talking about me tonight, get with the program. It's your dream come true. Now, you were saying you talked to Dad about love?"

"Yeah."

"Talking to me about it when you think you love some guy isn't enough?"

"You aren't really that much help. Besides, I thought we were talking about you tonight. Fucking with the status quo."

"Oh, yeah. Do I really have to ask you to tell me what Dad said?" Sebastian polished off beer number five in one long swallow, leaning heavily on the counter.

"He said, yeah, he loved Mom. That he'd do it all over again even if the same thing happened."

"He would?" Sebastian's hand froze a few inches above the counter, but the empty bottle kept going, falling on its side with a clunk, then lazily rolling away from him.

"Yeah. He said it was worth it. That it would have been even if they hadn't had us. He'd like to fall in love again."

"That's . . . informative. What else did he say?"

"He said when Mom first left him he felt like hamburger inside."

Sebastian blew out a breath. "Okay, so did this help you? What Dad said?"

"Yeah. When Alec dumped me, I didn't feel like hamburger. I felt more like, I don't know. Scrambled eggs."

"You know, you aren't that much help with my relationships, either. I feel like . . . dreck."

"Dreck."

"Dreck. Excrement. Worthless trash. I *hurt* him! He's too sweet to hurt."

"Dreck. Has it ever occurred to you that you're overeducated?"

"No. Dreck is perfect. It's what I am."

"I'm going to enjoy returning to the status quo."

Sebastian didn't answer because it sounded like Sophie was talking to herself.

She blew out a breath. Into the phone. It hurt his hearing. That called for another beer. "Okay, Sebastian?"

"Yes?"

"Is it possible you actually *do* love Brad?"

Sebastian stopped in front of the open fridge door, beer in hand. "I don't know." He stared at the asinine poetry magnets Paul had bought. How poetic. "Dreck" and "love" were both right in front of his face.

How *did* he feel about Brad?

He decided to start with the physical stuff, first. It was the easiest for him. 'Sides, they had a primarily physical relationship, right? Might need to warn Sophie of rough seas ahead. "Kay, this is going to be about sex. Superlative sex. Write that down. And 'best ever.'"

"Wait. I'm your secretary now? Christ. Hang on a second," Sophie grumbled, but he could hear the scratch of pen on paper.

"Thank you, dear sister."

"Okay, I have a feeling I'm going to regret this, but why was the sex so great? Brad was basically inexperienced, with men at least, when you guys got together. Was it because you taught him how to do everything? Please feel free to be vague with details."

"I didn't teach Brad how to kiss. And sometimes when we were kissing . . ." Shivers ran up Sebastian's spine, remembering what it was like to kiss Brad that first time he'd seen him after being apart a while. "Fantastic kisser. Write that down." His voice dropped to a scratch. "Who do you think Brad will be kissing next?" The ache in his chest knifed him. He flinched.

"It's pointless to think about," Sophie said, voice hard, "because whoever it is isn't any of your business, right? We need to get back to this list."

Sebastian swallowed. "Okay. Hang on." Other than kissing, what was it like to be with Brad? Sebastian closed his eyes and remembered. Sometimes when they made love, he felt like he was part of Brad. Like nothing separated them. Not even skin. "Write this down: 'We made love.'"

She sucked in a breath, but he could hear the pen again.

Who was Brad going to make love with next?

He doubled over when the image of Brad with his roommate Collin popped into his head.

"*Made love*," Sophie breathed.

"I'm starting to get the feeling I'm a gigantic dumbass who's missing something important. And possibly obvious."

"Me too. The dumbass part."

Dad had told Sophie stuff about what love felt like. What was it? Fireworks, right? Love was supposed to be like fireworks. Sebastian took a deep breath and closed his eyes, hearing Brad's voice. *You know I'm in love with you, right*?

He almost jumped out of his skin when the first bottle rocket took flight in his chest.

"Fuck. I have to go." He hung up on her response, which sounded like it rhymed with "Dumbass," and scrambled for his clothes. Something else in his chest was making like it was going to explode now, but it was the sucky, I-fucked-up kind of explosion. The kind where you accidentally cut the blue wire instead of the red one.

He had to find Brad. It was Saturday night. Brad would be at that pledge ceremony thing, right?

Should he wait? His heart was screaming at him to go *now*, before it was too late. Before he lost any more time. Before Brad decided he was better off without Sebastian. Go there and wait for Brad if he had to.

Would that look bad? He'd already fucked up enough today. He didn't want to make it worse by inadvertently outing Brad, but . . . He didn't think Brad was coming back here, so it was the frat or nothing.

Besides, he was Brad's tutor. Guys' tutors stopped by the frat occasionally, right? And waited hours for them to show up if necessary.

On Saturday night.

Sure.

Didn't matter. He had to go *now*.

Chapter 38

It was almost time. *El Presidente* Eduardo droned on about frat business in the front of the room, holding his silly little gavel prominently. Collin sat on Brad's left, twisting his fingers. What did they call that? Wringing his hands. Kyle sat to his right, his knee going up and down a mile a minute, tightly clutching his notecards.

Brad was starting to wonder if *they* were going to come out tonight, too.

Although really, there was just no way Kyle was gay. Not even bi. Brad was betting Kyle was one of those guys on the extreme hetero end of the spectrum. In spite of his weird curiosity about gay sexual practices.

Eduardo wound his way through all the damn Theta Alpha Gamma business, discussed the new pledges, and now finally, finally, was getting to the New Business.

"We only have a few minutes before our newbs show up to begin the initiation rites." This was met with a series of catcalls and cheering. Who didn't love to insult, abuse, and break the spirits of a bunch of guys who were basically begging for it? "Is there any new business? No? Then—"

Brad stood up. "I have new business."

The room quieted down and everyone turned to look at Brad. That "new business" thing was just a formality. Nobody was actually supposed to pop up with any.

Eduardo sighed and set down the stupid gavel he'd gotten out of a gumball machine or wherever. He leaned heavily against his podium and waved at Brad to go on.

Brad opened his mouth and drew a breath, but before he could say anything, Kyle popped up. "Brad's gay."

Motherfucker.

The only thing to do was agree. "I'm gay." The sound of Collin swallowing echoed around the room. Brad glanced down at him. He was white as a sheet.

Eduardo looked a little pale himself. "Brad, Kyle is accusing you of being gay. Do you have any answer to this accusation?"

Kyle protested. "It's not an accusation! I'm *supporting* him!"

"I cannot believe Ashley loves you," Brad said out of the corner of his mouth, glaring sideways at Kyle. "Yeah, I do. I. Am. Gay."

Kyle swallowed, blanched, and sat down rapidly. But Brad was betting on a quick recovery. Not so much for the rest of the guys, who were all staring at him, some craning their necks or gape-mouthed, completely frozen. Still enough that he was starting to wonder if he'd turned them all to wax, like in one of those museums.

Eduardo shuffled papers up at his podium, nostrils flaring rhythmically. He tilted his chin at Brad. "So. You are supporting Kyle's assertion that you may be gay?"

"I just *said* I was gay," he said, flinging out a hand for emphasis. The waxen zombie horde flinched slightly.

Kyle stood up next to Brad again. "It's true. Brad's gay. He even has—*had* a boyfriend."

Fastest recovery on record. Brad shot Kyle another dirty look. Kyle ignored him this time, instead staring menacingly at Eduardo.

Eduardo's eyes bounced around the room like he was looking for backup. When he found none, he squared his shoulders and asked evenly, "Are you sure you are gay? Maybe you're just confused."

"I'm not *confused*, Eduardo, I'm gay."

Eduardo swallowed, his shoulders hunching slightly. "Ah. Have you . . . conducted any tests to prove this theory?"

For fuck's sake. "It's not a fucking theory. And yes, I've sucked cock."

That woke everyone out of their zombie state. A chorus of "Dude!" and "Oh, man, that's just gross," erupted.

Eduardo banged his silly little gavel until the head broke off, trying to get everyone to shut up. It took a few minutes and a piercing whistle from Tank, but they finally fell quiet. Eduardo turned back to Brad. "It's not funny to pretend you're gay if you're not. It's insulting to the real gay men."

Okay, that was it. What was with people thinking he had some amazing sense of humor? He glared at Eduardo. "If you don't shut the fuck up, I'm going to insult your real straight ass."

That didn't come out quite the way he'd meant it to.

Everyone went very still again, teetering on that edge of disbelief. Finally, he was getting somewhere. He waited for the questions to begin. Everyone would have something to say to him, he was sure.

They all started talking at once. To each other. Mostly about whether Brad was fucking with them, and how he'd gotten Kyle in on it with him. *Shit.* There was no fucking way he was letting them derail his coming out, dammit. *"Quiet!"*

Silence.

The doorbell echoed through the house.

Julian popped up and planted his hands on his hips and yelled, "Goddammit! If that's some pledge arriving early, I'm blackballing him, plumbing experience or not!"

Everyone started talking again. As the discussion—the very loud, chaotic discussion—raged on, Brad began to get really, really pissed off.

"You guys are ruining my coming out!" he finally yelled.

No one heard him but Collin. Collin, the only guy in the entire room who wasn't standing up and yelling. He looked miserable when Brad turned to him. "Sorry," Collin croaked, looking like he was going to faint. Kyle, meanwhile, was yelling at the top of his lungs about discrimination and lawsuits, reciting things from his notecards.

Brad reached down and squeezed Collin's shoulder. "You'll do it when you're ready." Collin slumped in his chair.

Brad looked around in disgust. The debate was turning into a big argument. First stop on the way to a brawl. Eduardo waded his way toward Brad. "You can't be gay," he insisted once he was in shouting distance. "You're too macho!"

Ricky, standing nearby, overheard and butted in. "You've been with *girls*, dude."

"You don't seem gay to me," Eduardo added.

"Well, shit! I don't seem gay to you? My mistake, then," Brad said with an eye roll.

Eduardo held himself straighter. "There's no call for sarcasm."

Yes. Yes, there was, actually. He was about to tell Eduardo just how much call there was for it when someone said from behind him, "But I looked up to you, man! I thought you were the shit when it came to the ladies. So, what? Am I going to wake up gay one day, too?"

Brad closed his eyes and rubbed a hand across his face. "Please, tell me you guys are not seriously this stupid."

But no one was listening to him. Again. They were arguing the possibility of waking up gay one morning. Brad didn't know what the fuck to do. He'd been prepared to defend his right to stay in the frat once he was out, maybe even to have to answer a lot of stupid questions like he had for Kyle. He hadn't been prepared for no one to believe him. Or for idiots to think it was some kind of contagious social disease.

He dropped back into his chair. "This is a fucking disaster." Collin nodded his head glumly but didn't say anything.

Just then Julian reappeared in the doorway, someone following him.

Brad stood up. It was Sebastian, which made absolutely no fucking sense. He was looking around worriedly. Then he saw Brad and smiled, just a little. A kind of unsure one that Brad had never seen on his face before.

Shit. Brad's heart flew up his throat at the sight of it. The fuck did that smile mean? And what if someone figured out he was the guy Brad had been seeing and they started harassing Sebastian? What if it got physical?

He started toward Sebastian, trying to get to him before something went horribly wrong. He could hear snippets of arguments on the way. "Dude, does it really matter if he's gay? So what? You're an asshole and I don't hold it against you."

"No, see, it's a good thing. Chicks *love* gay guys. We'll have women here 24/7."

"Gay or not, he can still kick your ass."

"My brother's gay. If you think I'm coming down on Brad for being gay, you're smoking." The last comment was from Tank. Brad nearly stopped to thank him. If he had Tank on his side, no one would touch Sebastian.

Brad was so fucking relieved it wasn't a gay bashing in the making, he smiled at his boyf— ex-boyfriend.

That's when Sebastian really let loose. He smiled back so big it lit up his whole face. Brad stopped, brought to a standstill by that smile. His breath stuttered in his lungs. It looked like . . . was Sebastian here to see *him*?

Brad must have had some weird look on his face, because Sebastian slowly lost the smile. He looked worried now. Looking into Brad's eyes. Trying to figure something out.

Brad pushed closer through the guys, wanting to know just what the actual fuck Sebastian was doing here, anyway.

It only took a few seconds before Brad was standing in front of him.

"What's going on?" Sebastian asked, taking a deep breath.

Brad looked around, then met Sebastian's gaze "I came out."

Sebastian's eyes widened, but he just nodded. "Um, how's that going?"

Brad glanced at the arguing mob again. "Not that great. No one believes me. Well, not no one, but not a lot of them."

Sebastian reached out for his hand. "They can't process it, yeah?" he asked, squeezing Brad's hand. Brad stared at it. Sebastian's hand wrapping around his.

"No. I don't get it. Look at them, they're still arguing about it," he said absently, staring at where Sebastian's skin met his. Then he pulled his hand away because he didn't know what it meant and it hurt to have Sebastian touch him. "Just . . . they don't believe me."

"I think that sounds like their problem."

Everything went still. Well, not really, but that was how it felt. It *was* their problem. He sighed with some weird mixture of resignation and relief. Whatever; it wasn't his deal anymore.

"Can we go talk somewhere?" Sebastian asked, voice so low Brad had to lean forward to hear him.

Brad swallowed and nodded. "We can go up to my room and talk."

Chapter 39

As soon as Brad shut the bedroom door, Sebastian turned into him. He needed to be close to Brad. But Brad stepped away, across the room.

Sebastian stopped. He didn't know what to do with his hands. When was the last time he didn't know what to do with his hands? He clasped them in front of him. Gripped them together. The ache in his chest grew. Telling him not to fuck this up. He had to clear his throat before he could speak. "Hey."

Brad looked at the floor, his jaw clenched. Maybe he wasn't going to answer. Damn it, it was worse than Sebastian had thought. The pain under his sternum throbbed.

"So you told the frat, yeah?" *Obviously, asshole.* He didn't know where else to start.

Brad nodded at the floor. "Don't you want to know why?"

"I don't care why."

Pain flashed across Brad's face, twisting his mouth. *Oh, hell*—he took a couple steps toward Brad.

Brad took a step back.

"I didn't mean that, I mean, not the way it sounded. I meant it doesn't matter if you came out or not, or why you did it. It doesn't make any difference to how I feel about you." This time when he stepped forward, Brad didn't back up. But he wouldn't look at Sebastian, either.

Sebastian watched Brad's Adam's apple work. "How's that?" Brad's voice shook, and Sebastian swore it hurt Brad to force it out.

"I love you, Brad."

It came out easier than he'd thought it would. Just flowed right out. He hadn't even had to think before he said it.

He didn't get the reaction he expected, though. Brad still wouldn't look at him. "If you're just saying that . . ."

He tried another step forward. "Why would I lie about that?"

Brad shrugged, looking sadder. "This morning you didn't know what love was."

Oh. Yeah. Sebastian stopped inching forward and cleared his throat. "I figured it out."

Silence. He held his breath. Brad lifted his head, not quite looking at Sebastian yet. "You did?"

Sebastian took another step. "Yeah. Love feels like a hole in my chest when you're gone. When you left me, I mean." Another step.

Brad smiled a tiny, sad smile. "That sounds familiar."

"Yeah?" Sebastian finally reached Brad's personal space. Less than a foot away. He could feel Brad there, physically feel him. His heat.

Brad peeked up at him from under his brow. "Yeah." He was so freaking cute when he did that.

Sebastian bent his knees to put himself into Brad's line of sight. "Familiar how?"

Finally, finally Brad reached for him. Just a quick touch of fingertips on his jaw before he dropped his hand. "That's how I felt when I left."

Sebastian reached for Brad's hand and pulled him closer. Brad came, meeting his eyes. Sebastian traced his cheekbone with his free hand. "I love these bones."

Brad frowned. "*That's* what you love about me?"

Sebastian palmed the back of Brad's head and brought him closer. "I love everything about you. I'm in love with you."

Brad resisted his hand, not letting Sebastian kiss him yet. "Are you sure?" The catch in Brad's voice nearly broke his heart.

"Yeah, honey. I'm sure. I don't know that much about it, yeah? So I didn't recognize it until after you left. I don't . . . please don't do that again. I wanna talk about problems, yeah? I want you to tell me what's wrong. I *love* you."

Brad whispered, "Okay," and let Sebastian pull him down for a kiss.

But Sebastian only got a quick one. Well, not that quick, but shorter than he expected by far. Then Brad pulled away, saying, "I want to talk now."

Sebastian pulled back himself, but didn't let go of Brad. "Okay," he whispered, stretching for another quick kiss. "Let's talk now."

Brad cleared his throat. Still skittish. "'Kay."

Sebastian pulled on his hand, leading him to the bed. They sat on the edge, and he toed off his shoes. Brad opened his mouth, then he closed it. He did it a couple of times before Sebastian said, "Can I hold you, hon? I'll lean against the headboard." He couldn't stop himself from running fingers through Brad's hair and along his cheekbones. He thought maybe Brad could say whatever he needed to say if he didn't feel like Sebastian was watching him.

Brad turned to him, startled. "Yeah."

So Sebastian sat against the headboard, making room between his legs for Brad. He was a few inches short for this, but that just put him at the right height to kiss Brad's spine. He squeezed his arms around Brad's chest, forehead on the nape of his neck. "I can't believe I almost let you go."

"If I hadn't left, what do you think would have happened?" Brad asked, running his fingers up and down Sebastian's feet.

"I don't know."

"But do you think you would have figured out how you feel?"

"I don't know." And he didn't really like to think about it. He kissed Brad's neck. "I know it would have taken me a lot longer to work it out, though."

Brad ran his index finger down Sebastian's instep. "How did you figure it out?"

Brad's neck needed another kiss. Sebastian sighed into his skin and rested his forehead on Brad's neck again. "Well, first I had most of a six-pack, yeah?"

"Yeah?" Brad whispered, tickling the soles of Sebastian's feet now.

He nodded. "Then I made a list."

Silence. Even the fingers stopped. Then Brad reached back and hooked a finger in the top of Sebastian's sock, pulling it off. "What kinda list?" He pulled off the other sock.

"I wanted to know what being in love was like, yeah? So I thought if I wrote down everything I felt for you and then embellished the feelings, that might tell me."

Brad's hands stopped moving. "Embellished them?"

"Like, enhanced them. Magnify them as much as I could."

"Huh." Brad's hands started moving again, fingertips tracing the bones of Sebastian's feet. Sebastian squeezed Brad tighter.

"So, I made a list. But there wasn't any way to make the stuff on it *more*. I don't think it's possible . . . I mean, I don't think things get more intense than this, hon. The things on the list . . ."

"Like what?"

Sebastian took a deep breath. "Like when we make love I feel like we're melting into one person. Like when I imagine you in bed with someone else, I get physically ill. Like if you needed a kidney, I'd give you mine. Like if I could take away the pain I caused you today and suffer it for you, I would."

"All of that," Brad whispered. "I feel every one of those things for you."

Sebastian blinked rapidly, lashes leaving wet trails on Brad's neck. "Thank God."

Brad twisted his head and shoulders around to kiss him. He knew it was partly for comfort, but when Brad touched him, he needed him. Needed to be naked and have his hands on Brad, making him cry out his name.

He could barely pull back to speak against Brad's mouth. "Wanna make love to you," he panted.

"I want that, too," Brad breathed, lying back and pulling Sebastian on top of him.

Sebastian's breath kept hitching in his chest, and his fingers wouldn't work. He could hardly look Brad in the eyes; he felt too exposed. But Brad stroked Sebastian's back and got Sebastian's fly open and his own jeans down his thighs. Squirming a hand between them and holding their shafts together. Holding his jaw and looking at him.

Brad's hand felt . . . just . . . incomparable around them, holding them together. Sebastian rested his forehead on Brad's, cupping his face, stroking his cheekbones. Too uncoordinated to move. Unable to catch his breath. Brad's hand tight around both of them, making Sebastian's skin vibrate and excitement resonate through his balls and the pit of his stomach and up his back. Taking the ache he'd lived with most of the day and turning it into something else by the judicious application of friction.

"Brad," he panted. His hips remembered what to do, finally, and he ground against Brad. Brad brought his other hand up to Sebastian's jaw, tilted his head to the right angle. And then, just like every other time Sebastian had kissed him, Brad opened up for him, let Sebastian have his mouth. Moaned and arched into him when Sebastian swept in with his tongue.

Sebastian planted his knees on the bed and thrust against Brad's skin, working one hand under Brad to hold him at just the right angle. Forcing Brad's legs up. Brad's cockhead rubbed just above Sebastian's pubic bone, hot and getting slippery, and Brad was making those noises he made. Sebastian gripped him tighter, a finger slipping between Brad's cheeks. "C'mon honey," he panted. "Let me hear it, Bradley."

Brad tilted his head back, eyelids heavy, and Sebastian knew it was all over for him. He drove himself into Brad's skin once more and came. "Fuck, Brad," he whispered, "Need you."

He felt and heard Brad come with one of those cries he made, fingernails in Sebastian's back, cum on his ribs. Sebastian kissed him, hard and wide open, eating the noises Brad made.

They lay there panting a minute, but it wasn't enough. Sebastian slid down, pulling Brad's shirt up farther, over his head, and licked his skin clean.

Brad was still mostly hard, still breathing heavy. Sebastian sucked him into his mouth and gently coaxed him back to full hardness. He watched Brad's face, then his eyes when Brad shoved a pillow under his head to see Sebastian suck him.

Sebastian took his time, but eventually Brad was rocking his hips, mouth hanging open as he panted, on the edge of writhing. Sebastian massaged Brad's balls, slid his middle finger down to press on Brad's hole, and Brad came again, biting his hand to keep quiet.

Sebastian pulled himself back up to sprawl over a completely limp, warm, sated Brad. He kissed him, letting Brad taste himself in Sebastian's mouth. He pulled back, smiling at Brad's heavy eyes and flushed face.

He looked debauched, smiling lazily.

"I love you," Sebastian whispered, not willing to let Brad drift off yet.

Brad's smile got a lot less lazy. "I love you, too."

"Are you sure?"

Brad looked startled. "Of course I'm sure. I love you, Sebastian." He stretched up for a kiss. Sebastian followed him down and rested his head against Brad's.

"I'm sorry for what I put you through, honey," Sebastian whispered in his ear.

"I know. It's okay." Brad's arms tightened around him. "Whatever it took for you to figure it out."

"I believed you; that you loved me. I think I was scared."

"I was scared too," Brad whispered.

Sebastian rubbed his cheek against Brad's, listening to the scritching sound. "I'm sorry," he repeated because it seemed important. Brad squeezed him even tighter, turning his face to nuzzle his cheek. "If it makes it any better—" Sebastian paused to swallow "—it made me feel amazing when you told me. Nearly the best moment of my life."

Brad froze, nose against his cheek, chest tensing as he held his breath. Sebastian heard him lick his lips before he asked, "What's the *best* moment of your life?"

His heart thumped at him, terrified and elated. "This one."

Brad's breath escaped in a whoosh against his ear. "Mine too."

His pounding heart was now accompanied by his tremulous fingers in Brad's hair. "I have something else to talk to you about," he said against Brad's cheek.

"Hmm?"

Even though Brad wasn't watching him, he still had to squeeze his eyes shut before he could say, "Move in with me."

Oh, hell. That might have been better as a question.

Brad pushed himself up on his elbow, dumping Sebastian on the bed, to stare down at him "You want me to live with you?"

Sebastian unscrunched his eyes enough to try to read Brad's expression. Shock, but not fear. He sucked in a breath and forged on. "Yeah. I really, really want you to move in with me." He reached with trembling hands to cup Brad's face. "We'll just try it for the summer, yeah? See how it goes."

He could tell Brad later he wasn't allowed to change his mind.

Brad stared down at him, unblinking, as Sebastian's heart beat outside of his body, somewhere in the space between them. Brad drew in a shaky breath. "Are you sure? 'Cause I want to, but I don't know if I'll ever make myself leave."

Sebastian swallowed. "I'm sure. Tell me you'll live with me."

Brad smiled all at once—beamed at Sebastian, grabbing one of his wrists and holding tight. "Okay. I'll live with you. I'm staying here this summer. Professor Harris offered me a job. I can move in whenever—"

ohthankGod

"—She asked me a week ago, but I was kind of waiting to tell you. Sebastian?"

Sebastian swallowed. His shaking had built up to nearly seismic proportions when Brad agreed. He probably looked sick to Brad, but he could feel a smile starting to take over his face. A tear he hadn't even known was there rolled down his temple, and he had to let go of Brad with one hand to swipe at his eyes, making an effort to get himself under control. "Toby will go home for the summer, but he'll pay rent to keep his room in the apartment. Once I kick Paul out, we'll have it to ourselves. Then maybe in the fall we can get our own place, yeah?"

"You're kicking Paul out?"

"Paul's an asshole to my boyfriend. That's unacceptable."

"Can you just do that, though? Kick him out?"

Sebastian shook his head. He didn't care about "can." "My name's on the lease; his isn't. So, yeah, I think I can. God, Brad, I fucking want you there so much I don't care. We'll move now if that asshole won't. Just live with me."

Brad leaned his head against Sebastian's palm, nuzzling it, then cupped one side of Sebastian's face, thumb tracing his lips. "Think of all the things we can do if we have that place to ourselves."

"All the time we can spend together. Yeah." Sebastian couldn't wait anymore. He pulled Brad down for a kiss. A hard, possessive, possibly frantic kiss. Brad let him get it out—all the emotions he'd worked up in the last few minutes—let Sebastian have his mouth and his tongue and whatever he needed. Giving himself.

Sebastian almost let it get out of control, but he didn't want to make love in Brad's frat again. He ended the kiss. "Let's go home," he whispered against Brad's temple.

Brad smiled against his chin. "Yeah. I want that. Let's go."

Explore more of Theta Alpha Gamma at

riptidepublishing.com/titles/universe/theta-alpha-gamma

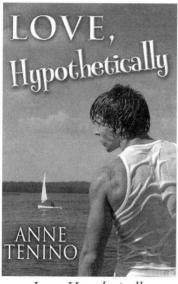

Love, Hypothetically
ISBN: 978-1-937551-50-6

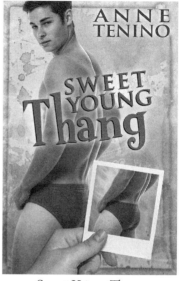

Sweet Young Thang
ISBN: 978-1-62649-033-8

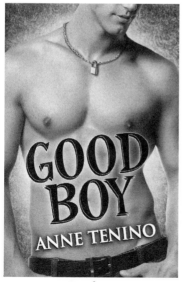

Good Boy
ISBN: 978-1-62649-068-0

Poster Boy
ISBN: 978-1-62649-131-1

Dear Reader,

Thank you for reading Anne Tenino's *Frat Boy & Toppy*!

We know your time is precious and you have many, many entertainment options, so it means a lot that you've chosen to spend your time reading. We really hope you enjoyed it.

We'd be honored if you'd consider posting a review—good or bad—on sites like **Amazon, Barnes & Noble, Goodreads, Twitter, Facebook**, **Tumblr,** and your blog or website. We'd also be honored if you told your friends and family about this book. Word of mouth is a book's lifeblood!

For more information on upcoming releases, author interviews, blog tours, contests, giveaways, and more, please sign up for our weekly, spam-free newsletter and visit us around the web:

> **Newsletter**: tinyurl.com/RiptideSignup
> **Twitter**: twitter.com/RiptideBooks
> **Facebook**: facebook.com/RiptidePublishing
> **Goodreads**: tinyurl.com/RiptideOnGoodreads
> **Tumblr**: riptidepublishing.tumblr.com

Thank you so much for Reading the Rainbow!

RiptidePublishing.com

RIPTIDE
PUBLISHING

Acknowledgments

I'd like to thank Dlee, Thorny and the Posse for all their help in shaping this book. A special thanks goes to Taylor V. Donovan for endless support.

Also by Anne Tenino

About the Author

Raised on a steady media diet of Monty Python, classical music, and the visual arts, Anne Tenino rocked the mental health world when she was the first patient diagnosed with Compulsive Romantic Disorder. Since that day, with her trusty psychiatrist by her side, Anne has taken on conquering the M/M world through therapeutic writing. Finding out who those guys having sex in her head are and what to do with them has been extremely liberating.

Anne's husband finds it liberating as well, although in a somewhat different way. He has accepted her need for "research" and looks forward to the benefits said research affords him. He thinks it's kind of cool she manages to write, as well. Her two daughters are mildly confused by Anne's need to twist Ken dolls into odd positions. They were raised to be open-minded children, however, and other than occasionally stealing Ken1's strap-on, they let Mom do her thing without interference.

Anne's thing is writing gay romance and erotica.

Wondering what Anne does in her spare time? Mostly she lies on the couch, eats bonbons, and shirks housework.

Check out what Anne's up to now by visiting her site, www.annetenino.com.

You can also find Anne at:
Chicks & Dicks (www.chicksndicks.blogspot.com)
Twitter (www.twitter.com/#!/AnneTenino)
Goodreads (www.goodreads.com/annetenino)
Facebook (http://on.fb.me/zyQEJP)

too STUPID to LIVE

It isn't true love until someone gets hurt.

Sam is too skinny, too dorky, too gay, and has that unfortunate addiction to romance novels, but he knows his One True Love is out there. He's cultivated the necessary fortitude to say "no" to the next Mr. Wrong, no matter how hot, exciting, and/or erotic-novel-worthy he may be. Until he meets Ian. Ian has escaped the job he hated and the family who stifled him, and is now ready to dip his toe into the sea of relationships. He's going to be cautious, maybe start with someone

who knows the score, nothing too complicated. Until he meets Sam. Sam's convinced that Ian is no one's Mr. Right. Ian's sure that Sam isn't his type. They can't both be wrong . . . can they?

Available at:
tinyurl.com/TSTL-Romance1
Ebook ISBN: 978-1-937551-84-1
Print ISBN: 978-1-937551-85-8

chapter 1

Ian Cully locked up his house—ex-house—one last time and contemplated throwing away the key.

Nah, quitting his job, selling his home, and moving the hell out of California was probably symbolic enough. Instead he just watched the brass glint in his hand. Then he stared at the deadbolt and the knob.

It isn't too late to go back to the department and drive a desk. That thought triggered a sudden and visceral flash of scraping his back on the asphalt and the sound of his skin sizzling.

Yeah, *fuck it.* He wanted the hell out of California. Wanted to live around family he *liked.* Put some distance between him and his dad.

"That's it?" his cousin Jurgen asked from behind him.

He should probably stop standing on his porch—former porch— staring at the locking hardware. "Uh, yeah."

"C'mon then. I want to get moving before dark." Jurgen's feet scuffed on the wood as he turned, and then Ian felt the boards give as he thudded down the steps.

He stared some more. Jurgen didn't say anything else, even though he was probably waiting by Ian's truck, back crammed full of stuff, ready to take off after the moving van that had left a half hour ago. Leaving the porch had been to give Ian space, although he knew damn well Jurgen wanted to get home to his boyfriend.

Still, Jurgen'd probably wait half the day if Ian needed the time.

Ian turned around, shoving the key in his back pocket, and headed down the stairs. Yeah, it was time to leave. Get rid of the last of the old life, because he was sure the hell ready for a new one.

When he reached his truck, Jurgen didn't move to climb inside. Instead he reached out and gripped Ian's shoulder too hard, pinching a nerve, but Ian didn't let himself flinch.

Jurgen looked him straight in the eye. "You're doing the right thing."

Ian nodded, held there by Jurgen's hand. "I am, yeah."

"Gets you the hell away from the chief."

Ian had to look away. "Yep."

If Jurgen didn't stop the personal sharing shit, Ian might have to rethink the moving near him thing.

Oh, wait. He was supposed to practice expressing his emotions now. He shoved his hands in his pockets and cleared his throat. "Yeah, uh . . . It was stupid, you know? The accident. But I guess it kind of straightened out my priorities." He stepped back from Jurgen, until his hand fell off Ian's shoulder.

Jurgen tipped his chin at Ian and turned toward the passenger door of the truck. That must have been enough bonding time for Jurgen. And thank God, it hadn't even been that hard. He could do this; all of it. No more being a firefighter, no more telling his dad he sometimes dated women, "just to make sure."

Yeah, the previous thirty-odd years hadn't worked out so well, but now he was pretty much free of that old life. Next step was to figure out what the fuck it was he actually *did* want out of the world. How hard could it be?

chapter **2**

Sam took a shortcut through a park located smack between the campus bookstore and his place, walking all over leaf-strewn grass he probably shouldn't have, clutching the book he'd hidden under his plaid shirt-jacket. He just needed to get to his apartment before he saw someone he knew.

If he ran into someone he knew, they'd expect him to stop and talk, because that's the kind of guy he was: the smiley, friendly, talky kind. Then, because he didn't have his backpack—*mental note, bring backpack next time*—they'd want to know what he was clutching away so furtively, *guiltily*, under his jacket. And—in spite of aspiring to an MFA in writing—he could never seem to come up with a plausible lie in truly dire situations.

At which point he'd have to make a break for it. Dammit, he was wearing those cool lumberjack boots he'd bought the last time he'd visited Nik in Whitetail Rock, and—newsflash—they sucked for running.

They looked good with plaid shirt-jackets, though.

A shouted "Hey!" interrupted his riotous thoughts.

He knew, he just *knew*, they were shouting at him. And he had a romance novel hidden under his shirt. A romance novel with a lurid cover featuring a bare-chested, kilt-wearing man on horseback, clutching a saloon-girl-cum-fair-maiden to his brawny chest.

"Hey! Get the hell off the field!"

Crap. Sam ran, hunching to protect the book, stumbling in an ungainly sideways sort of run.

He looked back over his shoulder. A whole pack of brawny Highlanders was chasing him. Sure, they had jeans on, and only some of them were bare-chested, but they all had that meaner-than-hell-Scot look in their eyes. It wouldn't have surprised Sam in the least if their knobby-yet-manly knees had been flashing under yards of plaid.

The leader of the clan made Robert the Bruce look like a little nellie boy. He was tall, thickly muscled, and light haired, with scruff Sam could see from ten yards away while running and looking backward over his shoulder. He had one of those brows that bordered on hairy Neanderthal, but somehow looked macho and sexy. His mouth was open, screaming some kind of battle cry, and he was gaining on Sam. Reaching out to grab him.

Sam slowed, considering the merits of letting the sexy Highlander catch him. Then his self-preservation instinct kicked in. He faced forward, clutched the book tighter, and put on some speed.

That was when some projectile clocked him in the back of the head. It nearly sent him into a somersault. His legs couldn't keep up with the forward momentum of his upper body. His knees gave and he pitched forward, throwing out his hands to catch himself.

Which was, of course, when he lost his grip on the book and dropped it. Actually, it was more of a fling than a drop. Sam lay there, cheek on the cold, damp autumnal grass, front getting soaked with dew, stunned and blinking at his book a few feet in front of him. *Verdant*, his brain supplied. *Your romance novel is lying in a verdant field of grass, longing for its reader.* A weird-looking, snub-nosed white football wobbled its way into his field of vision and came to a rocking halt.

Knees dropped onto the grass next to his head, jolting him. Sam strained his eyeballs upward and saw the brawny, shirtless Highlander who'd been leading the pack panting and scowling down at him. His sexy faux-Highlander muscles were straining and his chest was rising and falling rapidly. He had a veritable forest of caramel chest hair.

He made the best living, breathing (panting) romance novel cover Sam had ever seen. Macho and manly and stern and, *oh man.* Sam sighed. Guys like this were never gay. They were always the ones chasing the homos.

At that point it occurred to him to wonder why they'd been chasing him. "What are you doing?" he gurgled. His sluggish brain suddenly started calling out the anxiety attack.

The guy panted a couple of breaths before growling, "Playing smear-the-queer. Waddaya think? We're playing rugby!" He huffed derisively, then turned away. Sam saw him reach for the football, his hand hesitating over the book.

Oh, fuck my life. Sam scrunched his eyes shut. Other feet pounded up around him, and voices asked if he was all right and *What the fuck?* Sam held his breath, waiting for the shaming to begin.

When he felt something shoved roughly under his side, his eyes popped open, and he looked into the smiling, patronizing face of the Highlander. His fingers brushed against Sam's ribcage as he pulled his hand away.

Sam smiled tentatively. The Highlander shook his head in disgust, except he was smiling, just a little. "You all right?" he asked.

"Uh. Yeah." Sam stared dumbly. Was that a chorus of angels he heard? The sounds of the other players faded away as Sam met his Highlander's mossy green eyes. He felt a *something* lock into place inside his chest. *Click.*

Twue wuv.

It appeared to be a one-sided revelation.

His Highlander gazed back at him with some emotion in his eyes. It was . . . confusion. Confusion quickly becoming something more like condescension. He lifted his hand, still on his knees in the grass beside Sam, reaching for him as if in slow motion. Sam realized with horror that the Highlander was going to give him a conciliatory pat on the head and then stand up and walk away. Didn't he feel the *click*, too? How completely unfair that Sam should know instantly that this man was his destiny, but his stupid Highlander had no clue.

Poor, naïve hero. He wouldn't know what hit him when he finally fell in love. Sam almost felt sorry for him. Almost. It was hard to feel sorry for some bastard who was about to pat your head and dismiss you, soul mate or not.

"Ian!" One of his Highlander's clan, um, teammates was suddenly standing there, shaking the Highlander's shoulder.

Ian. His name is Ian. Sam sighed.

The Highlander—Ian—dropped his hand and looked away from Sam. "Yeah?"

"C'mon, man, you gonna play or what?"

Ian looked back at Sam for a second. "Yeah. Just give me a minute." The guys on the team started to wander away while Ian reached again for Sam.

At first Sam thought he was going to get the head pat after all, but Ian held out his hand, palm up. As if he wanted Sam to take it.

Sam stared at the hand a second, then looked back up at Ian. He was an ideal romance novel hero, in Sam's humble (yet well-read) opinion. All those muscles and that curly hair on his chest. Sprinkles of gold above his nipples, thicker on his massive, blocky pectorals. Who knew blocky was so hot? *Guh.* The hair, though. Sublime. Thinner on the sides but growing in toward his center, a line of it defining his sternum, swirling around his navel, arrowing toward his groin. *Happy trails to you . . .*

Ian snorted out a laugh, and Sam jerked his head off the ground. Ian was laughing at him, one side of his mouth curled up.

Oops. Sam might have let the ogling get out of control.

"You need help getting up, or what? C'mon, we wanna play." In a lower voice, he added, "Put your eyes back in your head."

Oh. Sam felt his face get hot as he reached out and took Ian's hand. The way this was going, it would be his only chance to touch his Highlander. Ian pulled him up so fast, he went from prone to standing with no stops in between.

"Jeez, you're strong." *And you, Sam, are a conversational reject.*

Ian just snorted that laugh again and looked at him. Standing, they were about the same height. That was kind of unusual. It made Sam's insides clench.

"You all right, kid?"

Kid? Oh! A pet name. "Um, yeah, think so."

"Let me see your eyes," he said, getting in Sam's face. Sam swallowed and held his breath while Ian scrutinized him carefully for something. Studying his eyes. They *were* his best feature, which wasn't saying much in his opinion. He'd never had someone pay quite this much attention to them, though. "Yeah," Ian muttered. "Same size."

"Uh . . .?"

"Your pupils. That ball hit you pretty hard. You might want to go to urgent care and get your head checked out, but you look all right to me." Ian shrugged, then added, "Not that I'm a professional."

"Oh." *Sparkling small talk, there.* "Um, my name's Sam."

Ian looked smirky, but held out a hand for him to shake. "Ian."

"Yeah, I caught that. Um, you know . . ." The blood started pounding in Sam's ears. Was he really doing this? He pretty much had to; it was the job of any successful romance protagonist. Sam wanted to be a successful romance protagonist, especially in this particular plotline. "Why don't you let me buy you a cup of coffee or something? Kind of a thank you."

Saying thank you with coffee. All the best heroes did it.

Ian eyed Sam, suddenly cautious. "What makes you think I'd be into a date with a guy?"

The click. "Oh, uh . . . Straight guys don't usually realize when I'm, you know, um . . . when I'm checking them out." Sam waved at Ian's naked, sculpted, hairy chest. *Yum.* "Or they get all, you know . . ." Sam bared his teeth and faux-growled instead of continuing.

You are such a dork.

"True that." Ian looked away from Sam, crossing his arms over his chest. Oooh, veiny forearms, and biceps like citrus fruits. Sam stared, and Ian finally said in a low voice, "Listen, kid, you're not really my type. Sorry, but . . ." He shrugged.

Sam's stomach bottomed out. He couldn't quite meet Ian's eyes. "Oh, that's not—I mean, I didn't figure I was, just . . . I really wanted to say thank you." Jesus, getting shot down was excruciating. It had never happened to him before. Probably because he'd never asked anyone out before.

It was unlikely he would in the future, either, based on this experience.

"There, you said it. You're welcome. Now go get checked out. And don't forget your book." Ian looked back down on the ground, where the impression of Sam was still fresh in the grass. His romance novel lay about where his heart had been.

Sam felt his face go redder. He bent over and snatched up the book, tucking it into his jacket. "Thanks," he mumbled, not looking at Ian. Shot down and humiliated. Twice.

Ian laughed shortly. It wasn't a mean laugh, exactly. Just a sardonic one. "You're welcome. Go on, Sam." *My name, he said my name.* "And stay off the field from now on, okay?"

Sam watched him walk off. He only meant it to be a glance, but Ian's back was mesmerizing. Yeah, he was sexy, but his skin was a mass of shiny smooth splotches mixed in with swirling scar tissue below his shoulder blades, all the way down, disappearing into his jeans. Three or four different shades of pink and tan. Parallel to his spine just above the small of his back was an incision scar. Dark brown and graphic, maybe five inches long.

Oh! My Highlander's been wounded. A scarred man, looking for the one person who can help his heart heal.

Sam caught himself before he clutched his chest from the angst of it all. He was a fool. A geeky, not-very-attractive fool. A too-tall twink of a fool who didn't get the time of day from hot muscle bears. If he were cute and small and blond (as opposed to towering, underweight, and bland), maybe Ian would want to tie him up and have his way. But Sam wasn't.

He looked down sadly at his book, then covered the heroine's face and most of her cleavage with his thumb and gazed at the Highlander beside her. He seemed so two-dimensional.

Duh.

Just you and me, buddy. You're all the Highlander I'm gonna get.

"Hey, kid!" someone shouted. "Get the hell off the field!"

Dammit.

Ian wasn't into pale, weak guys. Guys with no muscles and too-long, shaggy, wispy hair and blond eyelashes that disappeared unless they were in full sunlight. Long, coltish legs didn't do it for him, either. The fuck *were* coltish legs, anyway? Other than too damn skinny.

Ian liked muscular, barrel-chested, built-like-a-fireplug guys. With dark hair and a five o'clock shadow at 10 a.m.

Most importantly, he liked guys who were shorter than him.

Didn't he?

He shook his head at the memory of the kid making that awkward come-on. Maybe Ian had shot him down kind of hard, but you had to be cruel to be kind. And hell, he didn't have time to try to figure this out, he had too much other stuff to work on.

Tierney calling out to him brought his attention back to the present. He broke into a jog to get back into the game.

Weird how he could still feel the imprint of the kid's hand in his.

Want to read more of *Too Stupid to Live*?
Visit tinyurl.com/TSTL-Romance1

SWEET YOUNG Thang

When Plan A fails, turn to Man A.

Thanks to Collin Montes, Theta Alpha Gamma now welcomes gay and bisexual students. Enter repercussions, stage left: someone rigs the TAG House water heater to launch through the ceiling, then plants a bomb—thankfully unsuccessful—in the fraternity's basement. Paramedic Eric Dixon can't stop thinking about the kid he met during a call at his former college fraternity house. The age gap between them is trumped by sexy eyes, so when Eric sees Collin again at the bomb scene, he pursues him.

Soon, Eric is dreaming of being a househusband, fighting to keep Collin safe from whoever's trying to destroy the fraternity, and helping his sweet young thang realize that repercussions sometimes have silver linings.

Available at:
tinyurl.com/SYT-TAG3
Ebook ISBN: 978-1-62649-032-1
Print ISBN: 978-1-62649-033-8

RIPTIDE PUBLISHING

Chapter 1

"I'm probably going to die, aren't I?"

Eric Dixon fiddled with his patient's IV for a few seconds, collecting his thoughts. Mr. Siskin was on a fair amount of pain medicine, but his speech seemed clear. Eric met his gaze. "Do you remember what I said the problem was?"

Siskin grimaced. "Uh . . . aneurysm in my abdomen, right?"

"Well, that's what I think, but we don't carry the equipment on the ambulance to know for sure." Not to mention he wasn't a doctor. Eric watched the pulsing swelling just below Siskin's navel and could only imagine that was one thing, though. "It's called a thoracic aortic aneurysm. It means your aorta—the main artery supplying blood to your body—is in danger of rupturing. If I'm right, and that happens, you'll bleed to death." So fast that even if he was already in surgery and opened up, they might not be able to save him.

"How much danger?"

Eric blew out a breath. "You hear the sirens?"

Mr. Siskin nodded tightly. Sweat beaded on his forehead.

Eric leaned forward to adjust the drip, giving his patient more medication. "We don't always go to the hospital code three, meaning with the lights and sirens on. Only when someone's in imminent danger of death or permanent injury."

Mr. Siskin nodded again, closing his eyes. Maybe he believed in the power of prayer. Eric hoped it'd work, because there was nothing he could do except keep the patient as comfortable as possible. This sort of call frustrated the crap out of him. In this case, Lincoln's job—getting them to the fucking hospital as fast as he safely could—was the more important one.

Lincoln's job was extra hard today, though, because the Siskins had been vacationing at their cabin up on the McKenzie River, right at the border of their ambulance service district. Eric glanced at his watch. Best-case scenario, ten more minutes to the hospital.

Crap, he should have fucking called for a helicopter. But no, it wouldn't have been any faster. He'd had Siskin nearly ready to go when the swelling in his abdomen had started. One of those cases where even though the patient had shown signs of a heart attack, the EKG hadn't backed up the diagnosis. Eric'd had a bad feeling, and he and Lincoln had to take the guy in anyway, so they'd been working fast.

Siskin flinched, grimacing again. Even though his eyes were closed, when Eric reached for the IV again, he said, "No."

Eric looked down at him. "How bad is the pain? Remember the pain scale? Give me a number between one and ten—"

"I don't care." Mr. Siskin waved him back. "I don't want to die while I'm stoned." He smiled for a split second. "More stoned, I mean."

"Gotta tell you, Mr. Siskin, in my professional opinion, you need to believe you're going to live." He'd seen some people who should be dead refuse to die, and he'd seen a few who had no medical reason to die go ahead and do it.

"Call me Bryson."

"I can only do that if you promise me you'll live."

Siskin's eyes opened again and he actually grinned. Not for more than a couple of seconds, but he met Eric's gaze and shared a moment of humor.

Humor is a good thing. Eric smiled back, trying to make it genuine.

"Okay, it's a deal." Siskin sucked in another breath. "What's your name again?"

"Eric. At work, people call me Dix."

"Okay, Eric, I'm a numbers man. My whole career is about numbers—I'm an actuary for an insurance company. What are my odds of living? Give me a number."

"I really don't know," Eric said, relieved he didn't have to lie. "We can't know how bad things are without a CT scan, and I couldn't guess how much time you have before it ruptures even if we did."

Siskin looked at him levelly. "If it ruptures while I'm still in this ambulance . . ."

Crap. He nodded.

Siskin closed his eyes again. His breathing had evened out. Eric thought their discussion was over, but Siskin asked, "Do you have any kids?"

He knew—and hated—where this was going. "No, I don't. I'd like some, but it hasn't worked out."

Siskin grabbed his hand and gripped it tighter than Eric thought he could. "I have a son, you met him up at the cabin. If I don't make it, you tell him having him was the smartest, best thing we ever did. Tell him not to wait to give his mother grandchildren, more than one. Then tell him to take all the damned money I'm about to leave him and do something stupid with a little of it."

"I will. Promise." He craned his head, looking through the front seats to see out the windshield. "But we're nearly there. You can tell him yourself."

Siskin scrunched his brow. "Well, I can't tell him if I don't die, because I'm not giving him the damn money then."

Eric blinked. "I meant tell him how you feel."

Siskin nodded, and Eric could read the pain in his expression. Not the physical kind—the kind that made his whole face draw in, as if fighting to keep something from getting out. "I'll tell him, I gue—" He gasped, eyes opening wide and face paling.

Fuckfuckfuck. There was nothing he could do. Eric leaned closer, still holding his patient's hand. All Siskin's fear of dying that he hadn't shown before now welled up. Looking into his pupils felt like staring out into space. "I'll tell him, Bryson," Eric said.

Siskin licked his lips. "Do that."

"It's okay." Death. Death was okay, if you accepted it.

"Seems l-like it might b—" Siskin sucked in another quick breath, shaking with it, but he wouldn't ever get enough again. He was so pale now that Eric could see the black-blue voids under his eyes. He sucked in air once more, and squeezed Eric's hand reflexively. His body relaxed, and for a split second Eric could see the whole universe in his pupils, but all the stars were winking out one by one, until they dulled. Eric couldn't see in, and Bryson wasn't there to see out anymore.

Thank fuck. One of the better deaths.

Chapter 2

ollin held his cell phone to his ear, but was listening to the thoughts in his head rather than to his uncle.

For a young gay man like himself, college should be the best time of his life, right? He should do things with wild abandon; he should openly—publicly even—experiment with his sexuality; he should do stupid shit like light articles of furniture on fire and push them out of second-story windows; he should fail a class. Not get put on academic probation or anything, just flunk one measly economics class.

Which he was in danger of doing if he didn't pull at least a C on the midterm. And no, the first week of the quarter wasn't too early to start freaking out about that. He sucked at Econ.

He should have the freedom to flunk that damn class—to do all those things, and then laugh about them later (probably in some embarrassment) with friends who'd done equally stupid things.

Well, he had the friends part down cold; they came with the fraternity membership. Okay, and he'd made inroads on being a slut, but mostly in secret. But his stupid, overdeveloped sense of obligation had repeatedly kept him from pulling a variety of crazy, college-student capers. Obligation to his family, particularly his uncle.

The uncle he should probably be listening to, rather than daydreaming about throwing his desk through the window, soaking it in gasoline, and sparking it up.

"Now, Collin, I know you registered for that International Business Communications class, and I've been thinking it might make an excellent final project if you—"

Never mind, he didn't need to listen to Monty yet. He slumped further over his desk, resting his cheek on his fist, staring out at the gray, drizzly day. January was such a horrible time of year in Oregon. The month would totally benefit from a pile of furniture blazing merrily on the lawn.

Yeah. A raging fire would be an excellent way to dispel the current drizzle of life.

Instead, he had his uncle yammering in his ear about this term's courses and how each one was important to his future in the family business, including Econ. Or whatever.

"I think I've found a replacement for Sooty as liaison to the Alumni Weekend Committee," Uncle Monty said, snapping Collin back to attention. Well, for a moment, until Collin started wondering why they called the corporate realtor from Delaware "Sooty." Probably because at some Theta Alpha Gamma bacchanalia, he'd pushed a flaming sofa out a window.

Now Sooty was pushing up daisies, or would be in the near future.

Collin hadn't earned a nickname in college, not even once he'd joined the fraternity. It was probably for the best—he'd have ended up with a nickname like Jeeves, the Theta Alpha Gamma Butler. Or they'd name him after that kid in the Dutch fairytale that had held back the sea by sticking his finger in a dyke.

Not that Collin had any intentions of sticking his finger in any dykes. *Shudder*. But there was no denying he was the guy who always stepped up to the plate when no one else would. He felt like he managed the whole damn frat sometimes.

Okay, not the whole frat, but a lot of it.

Thank God Kyle had run for frat president for their senior year or Collin might not have escaped that fate.

"Collin, are you listening to me?"

He didn't even bother unslouching. "Of course I am, sir."

Julian acted far more like a frat butler than Collin ever had. Although, come to think of it, Jules's butlery was sort of a hollow performance. He posed as the guy who had his finger on the pulse of the place by answering the front door and dusting off random picture frames or the odd piece of furniture, but he was more footman than head of staff. If it didn't happen in the entryway, Jules didn't have a clue. He wouldn't survive a second belowstairs.

"... I've made reservations for you to play golf with him on Saturday morning. Seven a.m. at the McKenzie Club."

Collin sat up straight and nearly dropped the phone. "What?" *Him who*? Jesus, not Saturday morning. "Is it necessary for me to meet him so soon?" But more importantly, was it necessary for Collin to meet him on Saturday morning? Everyone knew Saturday morning followed Friday night, and if things went as hoped, he'd be sticky, sated, and sleeping at seven on any given Saturday. "Isn't it disrespectful to Sooty's memory to replace him so quickly? He only died a week ago." He cringed at using a dead man as an excuse, but it was necessary. Hopefully Sooty would understand. Collin had never met him in person, but a man who lit furniture on fire must realize the importance of Friday night.

"Sooty would have wanted it this way," Monty intoned.

Collin rested his forehead in his hand—the one not occupied with holding his phone—and massaged his temples. Could he possibly find a way out of this? "I'm sorry, but what time did you say I'm meeting, um, him, again?" He could have heard wrong.

"Seven." Monty must have swiveled around to stare out the windows overlooking his olive groves, because Collin could hear his uncle's chair making that familiar squeak. "Collin, as you know, I have a limited amount of time and I would appreciate it if you listened to me so I don't have to repeat myself."

"Sorry, sir." It was better to apologize and move on; experience had told him that.

"It's only golf, son. I know how you are about your Friday nights, so I didn't commit you to a dinner, which is what Sparky suggested."

"His name is Sparky?"

Monty sighed, and Collin flinched.

"It's Donald, but he earned the name Sparky in college and it stuck. After all, Sparky Donaldson is obviously preferable to Donald D. Donaldson." Monty paused before adding pointedly, "And you'll be meeting him at the McKenzie Club."

Collin fell back in his chair, holding in a groan. "Um, yes, I caught that part. But thank you." *For taking time out of your busy schedule to repeat it.* He cringed at the thought—he shouldn't think such disrespectful things about the man who'd all but raised him.

It probably wasn't a good sign that Collin had started reminding himself of that every time they spoke. *I love my Uncle Monty. I love my Uncle Monty. I lo—*

"I'm expecting a lot of you, I know, but I wouldn't give you such responsibility if I weren't confident you were capable of it. Once you've finished this chapter of your education and you take your position within the company, you'll appreciate these experiences. It's why I wanted you as the Theta Alpha Gamma alumni liaison. The position is very high profile, and as principal organizer of Alumni Weekend, you'll have the opportunity to make many valuable business contacts."

"Of course," Collin said, nodding into the phone.

"Now, as I said before, Sparky is only going to be in the Eugene area this weekend, and since he's available, I think a meeting would be advantageous."

Collin knew his uncle was only warming up to the topic, so he needed to ask what he wanted to know now. "Do you know how he got that nickname?" He figured it was the most pertinent information about the dude. Nicknames seemed very telling.

"Well . . . I shouldn't spread this around since it's unsubstantiated, but I've heard he was a bit of a firebug when he was younger. I've had quite a few business dealings with him, and he seems perfectly normal to me. Now, let me give you some more background—he's a very successful stockbroker, class of '86."

Collin's head began to fill with images of loud plaid golf pants, an engraved hip flask, and endless stories of a youngblood's early days on Wall Street. *Groan.* He couldn't keep his mind from drifting off again while Monty droned on, giving the socio-economic background of Sparky What's-his-name.

The dude sounded like a great time. Saturday morning was really shaping up to be lovely, wasn't it? Instead of sleeping off his bout of semi-anonymous sex, Collin would be blurry eyed on the golf course in freaking midwinter. "Sir," he said suddenly, seizing on that, "I'm sure you remember what Oregon can be like in January, are you certain—"

"I checked the weather report, and it's going to be clear. Brisk thirty-nine degrees, winds from the northeast. You'll be fine."

Shit, he was going to freeze to death. Dying at twenty-one, seated in a golf cart next to a corpulent moneychanger, wasn't how he'd imagined his death. He'd never imagined it, but if he had to, he'd prefer dying in his nineties, lying in bed beside a sexy, naked stripper in *his* twenties.

Monty cleared his throat, signaling an uncomfortable change of topic—one Collin thought he might benefit from listening to. "You should know Sparky is one of the alums who opposed the new membership policy."

Collin closed his eyes and counted to ten. "Uncle Monty . . ."

"I didn't deliberately set you up, Collin. He found out about Sooty passing on—they were friendly—and contacted me about taking the man's place. You know we need someone on that committee. The Alumni Weekend is coming up quickly, and you increase your chances of having a successful event if you work with more alums. And we both know the more alumni you impress, the better it is for you in the long term."

"It's not for twelve weeks. You can't give me time to find someone who isn't a homophobe?" *Oops.*

"Opposing the new membership policy does not make one a homophobe," Monty said curtly.

Oh God, headache. Right between the eyes. "Yes, sorry, sir." He needed to end this conversation, because he'd just implied that his uncle was a bigot.

"One might oppose this new 'open' membership policy because one feels, as do I, that it makes the fraternity a target. Especially since your friend is so publicly gay and continues to be an active member."

Collin sat up straight, matching Monty's tone and formality. "Please remember that, in fact, the fraternity has always accepted gay members because the policy didn't specifically exclude them. It was simply a tacit Don't Ask, Don't Tell system. We voted to codify the acceptance of those members, and show them that being out is acceptable and safe here at TAG." Monty could never seem to discuss just the policy; he had to make it personal by bringing up Collin's friend Brad. His uncle had been poking him with the pointy end of that argument since Brad had come out last spring, and it had worn right through his need to placate his uncle.

"That doesn't affect my opinion of it in the slightest. You persuaded me to accept this new policy by convincing me that it wouldn't alter the position of respect that generations of Theta Alpha Gamma brothers have worked to acquire at Calapooya College. I've placed my trust in you on this issue, and I interceded on your behalf with the Alumni Association members who questioned it as a favor to you. In return, I expect you and the other active brothers to ensure that TAG is just as influential on campus after this as it was before."

Collin swallowed, but used his "confident" voice. "I'm making certain of it, sir."

Want to read more of *Sweet Young Thang*?
Visit tinyurl.com/SYT-TAG3

Enjoyed this book? Visit RiptidePublishing.com to find more romantic comedy!

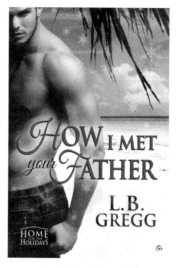

Apple Polisher
ISBN: 978-1-62649-035-2

How I Met Your Father
ISBN: 978-1-62649-084-0